PERFECT FAIRWAYS
HIDDEN LIES

A NOVEL BY

Robert E. Marier

Perfect Fairways...Hidden Lies

© 2018 by Robert E Marier

ISBN—978-0-578-41626-7

Robert E Marier
PO Box 2800
Kennebunkport, Maine 04046

Acknowledgements

After finishing the first draft of this mystery involving the world of golf, I had the pleasure and privilege of consulting with friend and noted Colorado educator Robert Burkhardt about the structure of the book and various concepts I had introduced. His pointed suggestions got me on the right track.

I then received the thoughtful and instructive opinions from one of my most admired and respected long-time Colby friends, consultant Edward Tomey from New Hampshire, whose comments caused me to deal with plot and character expansion issues. I hope I did so to his satisfaction.

Writer, illustrator and friend Steve Hrehovcik of Kennebunk, Maine, did much to move the book along through the editing process. His encouragement and guidance were much appreciated contributions.

Proof-reading and overview by Dr. Ken Janes of Kennebunk was essential to removing the unwanted and missing pieces involved with punctuation and grammar. He also provided the cover photographs for the book.

The encouragement from early readers, including John Raffaelli, James Thompson and Bob Gunter, kept fuel in my creative tank.

Finally, my deep appreciation goes to highly regarded free-lance writer, blogger and tolerant wife, Valerie Marier, who contributed the final and most significant edits to the book. Her suggestions as to word choice and sentence structure have made the book more readable and concise. Her efforts to drag me kicking and screaming from the world of storytelling to the necessary regimen of proper writing hopefully have struck a permanent chord.

Some things do take a village. I give you all a heartfelt thanks.

1

January 23, 2018

Detective Ben Angle of the Indio, California, Police Department was already having a bad day dealing with drug enforcement issues, but sometimes bad things come in bunches. When he went to room 328 of the Holiday Inn Express at 11:30 AM with his partner Shara Jones, he knew things had gotten a lot worse in this Southern California city.

The call from the desk clerk about a problem in one of the rooms was not out of the ordinary. The maid had attempted to clean room 328 but the "Do Not Disturb" sign hung on the door, so she waited until after the 11:00 AM checkout time before entering the room.

The fact that nobody responded when she knocked on the door was also not unusual. It happens all the time that people simply leave their motel when they pre-pay by credit card. The unusual thing was finding a beautiful blond girl lying in the bed. Dead.

Detective Angle immediately felt something was strange about this scene, especially when he could not see any signs of a struggle or any obvious marks on her body. She appeared to be about 25 years old, and physically fit. He thought it was unlikely this woman had suffered a heart attack.

The call by Shara to the County Coroner's office would bring help in about 30 minutes. In the meantime, Ben and Shara were careful not to disturb anything in the room or to touch the body or her belongings.

When they checked with the front desk, they learned that the room had been booked by an Amanda Joyal of Indio at 10:00 PM the prior night. Her car sat in the parking lot bearing a California license plate. Her cell phone rested on the bedside table.

Later that afternoon, after the body had been transported to the city morgue, Ben got a call from the coroner's office. Dr. Grant, the coroner, wasted no time filling him in.

"Ben, we have a weird one here," Grant said. "The cause of death is as clear as a bell. She suffocated."

"Well, we've seen that before," Ben said.

"Yeah," the Doc answered, "but here is the strange part— she had two golf balls stuffed in her mouth."

"What?" Ben gasped. "You're kidding me."

"Nope, and there's no doubt that with the balls stuffed in her mouth and her nose held closed, she'd take air in through her mouth and suck one of these balls into her trachea and be unable to breathe."

"That's a new one on me," Ben said.

Shara was astounded. "Why would anyone do that to a beautiful girl he had just met?"

Ben said, "Why does any sick person kill in the first place? There are millions of unpredictable reasons that float through the brains of crazies. That's the part that makes this kind of case so hard to solve. We've got to find out who this Amanda is, where she lives and works, and where she met the nut job who killed her.

"Shara, see what you can find out about her. Talk to her friends and employer. You know the drill. Also, notify her family. They'll know who she hangs around with. I'll start checking all the bars and other places where young people meet and hookup. This might be a love affair gone bad or an adulterous situation. Whatever, it's going to be tough to uncover."

"It's almost 5 o'clock, Ben, so I'll get at it first thing in the morning," Shara said.

Ben got a photo from the coroner but, because the girl had been in distress, it was not a good likeness. He needed to get a better one from her family or Facebook if he was going to discover who might have seen her in some bar. "We'll have to use this photo until we've talked with the family," Ben said.

Shara had some luck getting a fix on Amanda. The victim was a local girl who had attended USC and now worked as a sales manager for Salesforce, a large marketing and consulting company. Her parents were devastated. They gave Shara Amanda's graduation photo but otherwise were too overcome with grief to talk. A close friend said Amanda was 27 years old, easy going and fun to be with. Her friends thought she was determined to find a husband, and to have fun until she did. In both cases, a hookup in a bar that catered to her social type was the logical place to start.

With Amanda's photo in hand, Ben started to make the rounds of bars, talking to bartenders and waitresses. He found two places where Amanda had been seen, but not in recent weeks. No one remembered her being with any particular guy, but she was definitely part of the bar scene.

Finally, a bartender at the Nightfall Grill, the newest hotspot for young professionals to go, remembered seeing her on Monday night, just two days before. She was having a drink at the bar with a good looking guy in his mid-to-late 30's who he'd not seen before. Everything seemed normal. Ben said to Shara, "That was helpful, but who was the guy? Unless something jells, we are looking for a ghost."

January 30, 2018

Scottsdale, Arizona is a happening town. The winter season shifts into full swing when the sun-seeking snowbirds arrive in January. They fill the restaurants most nights, starting at "Early Bird" double drink time, and get replaced later in the evening with young people meeting and greeting, pairing up and lying to one another. It's a time when bad things can happen, but usually it's not murder.

Frank Larson had seen it all. Twenty-five years on the Scottsdale police force had hardened him to just about everything. Frank specialized in homicide cases and was good at it.

The call came in the early afternoon from the Roadhouse Inn. A maid had discovered a dead girl in the bathroom of room 450 when she went to clean the room. Frank and his partner, George Lappin, were not the first to answer the call, but they were experienced detectives and immediately took charge of the scene.

Nothing seemed to be disturbed in the room. The bed had been used but it was more pulled apart than as if someone had only slept in it. The woman's suitcase had been opened but nothing had been hung up.

The detectives found her naked body in the bathtub, which was still dry. No towels had been used. George and Frank knew well enough to not touch a thing. Frank went to the bedroom area to scope it out while George checked out the bathroom.

"Frank, come in here!" George shouted.

When Frank walked into the bathroom, George said, "Take a look at that," as he pointed to the girl's mouth which was partially open.

"What the hell?" he exclaimed, "is that a golf ball in her mouth?"

"It sure as hell is," George said, scratching his head. "And it looks like she may have choked on it. Let's get the coroner here real fast. This is weird."

The coroner arrived about 40 minutes later. Frank told him he wanted to go to the city morgue with him while he checked her out. He couldn't get his head around the golf ball thing, and wanted to get Dr. Epstein's take on the cause of death right away. There were no signs of foul play anywhere on the girl's body.

The coroner examined her arms and legs looking for injuries of any kind. Finally he looked at her head. He opened her mouth and, with eight inch forceps, extracted the golf ball which had been partly visible.

When he removed it, Dr. Epstein called Frank over and said, "Look, there were two golf balls pushed into her mouth. I thought I had seen everything, but this is a first."

Then he added, "If someone wanted to kill her, he sure found a unique way to do it."

They opened Mary Chapman's pocketbook and discovered her wallet, business cards and credit cards all untouched, including nearly $300 in cash. Robbery apparently wasn't the motive.

Chapman lived in Scottsdale and worked as a marketing director for a management company. The whole scene looked to Frank and George like a case of rape and a murder to cover it up. But the fact that there was no injury of any kind seemed puzzling.

She had booked the room herself, which meant she must have invited the assailant to her room. Frank said, "Maybe things got more serious, faster than she intended. Those golf balls would have kept her from yelling for help."

Frank took the bar/restaurant route the next day while George interviewed as many friends and co-workers as he could find. Her friends told him that Mary was not particularly fond of the bar scene but was hoping to find a mate. She wanted children and a normal family life. She held an enviable corporate title, but her goal was to become a wife and mother.

None of the bartenders who Frank spoke to recognized Mary as a regular customer. This was shaping up to be a tough case to crack.

February 13, 2018

Her whole life, Sherry White had wanted to be on the police force. Her father had been a detective until Parkinson's Disease forced him out at age 55. Her uncle, an "up and comer" on the force, was killed in his late thirties by some no-good kid trying to make it into a gang by knocking off a cop. This would have   discouraged many people but it only made Sherry more determined to tackle the job with enthusiasm and skill.

Working hard brought her to the detective level before her 40th birthday. She was quick-witted, intuitive and well liked. Her partner was a 32-year-old hotshot named Charlie Broms, a guy with perhaps too much chutzpah for his own good.

On a mid-February night they were cruising through the Brentwood area of Los Angeles, close to the bordering neighborhood of Palisades. It was early morning when they passed the Ramada Hotel. They spotted another cop car pull into the hotel driveway, probably responding to some kind of an emergency. Sherry stopped to check out the situation.

One of the hotel guests had asked for an early morning wake-up call. The guest also requested a "no fail" follow-up call because she was a deep sleeper and had an appointment she couldn't miss. When the desk clerk couldn't rouse the guest, he sent an assistant up to the room to make personal contact. After getting no response, the management decided to open the door.

They found a gorgeous woman laying at the bottom of the bed with her hands tied. Her empty eyes stared up at the ceiling and her mouth was wide open. She was dead. "Sherry, this is crazy," Charlie mumbled. "She has a golf ball in her mouth!"

After having the body processed, the coroner confirmed that there were in fact two identical Medallist golf balls stuck deep in the woman's windpipe.

Sherry's supervisor assigned her and Charlie to take charge of this case. She was determined to solve it, mostly because she hated to see the utter waste of a young life by some deranged maniac.

As it happened, Sherry had been researching a string of drug-related murders around Southern California a week or so before and had come across information about a bizarre death in the Indio/La Quinta area, about 130 miles away. The murder occurred on January 23rd. In reading the details, she discovered that the victim was also found with golf balls in her mouth.

Sherry told her partner about the case and mentioned that maybe they should get the FBI involved. "There's something very strange going on and it's somehow connected because of the unusual way these women were killed."

2

February 14, 2018

The next day Agents Joe Hancock and Paul Clark, of the Los Angeles FBI field office, arrived to meet with Sherry and her partner. Joe and Paul wanted to check out the scene and the body, and also talk to the coroner.

The coroner told them, "The cause of death was suffocation as a result of obstruction of the airway because of two golf balls forced into the throat."

As Joe studied the details of the case, he said to Paul, "This is too similar to the murder reported in Indio to be random." The public had not yet been informed about the cause of death in the Indio murder, so Joe knew it couldn't have been a copycat situation.

"We've got an unusual serial type murderer on the loose," he said. "I'm going to check out other areas in California and Arizona to see if other cases similar to this have occurred that we weren't notified about."

Sherry, pleased that the FBI had sent its top agents, said that she and her partner would do an exhaustive search of bars and restaurants in the Brentwood and Palisades area to see if anyone had seen the girl, alone or with a guy. "I'll also ask Charlie to check with her friends to determine her employment situation," she stated.

Later in the day, Agent Hancock sent out a blanket email to local and state police communication departments in adjoining states alerting them about the two recent murders involving young women in Southern California which had characteristics of serial killings. The FBI requested immediate notification of any similar crimes involving young women suffocated in an unusual manner.

Within an hour Agent Hancock received two emails. The first was from Ben Angle of Indio, and the second from Frank Larson of Scottsdale. They left their telephone numbers and said they wanted to talk to Joe without delay.

With curious anticipation, Hancock telephoned Ben Angle. "Hello Detective Angle, this is Agent

Hancock of the FBI. Thanks for responding to my email alert."

Angle responded, "We should thank you for putting out this alert because we have a case that is driving us nuts and the direction ahead doesn't look all that promising. We've got a girl who was killed by suffocation a few weeks ago, on January 21 to be exact. Can you believe that some sick bastard stuffed two golf balls down her throat so she couldn't breathe? There was no other injury to the body. He must have played games with her and then killed her in a way that wouldn't leave any clues, except the golf balls, of course."

"Ok, Detective, we've got a similar situation here in the Brentwood neighborhood of Los Angeles. Same MO. The woman was also killed by golf balls in her mouth. Out of curiosity, what kind of golf balls were used in the Indio murder?"

"Let me see, I'll have to check the evidence bag because I didn't pay much attention to the kind of ball. I'll be right back." A few moments later Ben picked up the phone again and said, "The balls were called Medallist Tour ZX."

"Are there any other marks on the balls?" Joe inquired.

"Yes, under the Medallist name is the number 77," Ben said.

"Hmm," Joe mumbled. "I'll be getting back to you. Oh, one more thing. Have you found any sign of a potential male subject?"

"The only clue, which might be important, was that one bartender claimed he saw her the night before she was found having a drink with a blond guy about her age, but it all looked normal. Other than that, we are just blowing in the wind," Ben said.

"Thanks, Ben, you'll definitely be hearing back from me soon."

Joe's next call was to Frank Larson in Scottsdale who had emailed about an hour earlier. "Frank, this is Agent Joe Hancock replying to you."

"Hi Joe, we've got a helluva dead-end mess here in Scottsdale. It's the damnedest strange thing. This beautiful local girl was found at the Roadhouse Inn laying in a dry bathtub, suffocated, and she was sucking on two golf balls, which I find very puzzling. We can't seem to make sense out of the whole thing because the young women was a refined kind of girl, according to her friends, and there was no apparent reason for anyone to have knocked her off."

"Well, Frank, I know that this will seem like an off-beat question, but did you happen to see what kind of golf balls were involved?"

"Yes, I did, I'm a golfer myself, so I notice things like that. It was a Medallist Tour ZX with an identification number of 77. That kind of ball is high-end and expensive, almost $5 bucks apiece. It is usually played by the more skilled amateur golfers and pros who are able to appreciate the nuances of a better ball."

"Ok, Frank, it looks to me that what we have here is some guy who travels a lot, plays golf well and has money to burn. Some guy who is a sick case and just wants sex and gets off by killing his victims. A nut job who can bury his tendencies until he hooks up with some unsuspecting young thing. This is not the last we will hear from him, I'm quite sure.

"By the way, did you speak to anyone who saw a man acting suspicious or different, who was just hanging around, perhaps a blond guy?"

"No, nobody we talked to," Frank said.

3

Sherry White had been sitting on pins and needles about this case. She knew Agent Hancock had sent out an email request for comments, hoping to get a response that would move the case along. She called him and was encouraged to hear there seemed to be a pattern to the killings. At the very least, that would give them all something to work with.

She asked to meet with the FBI team to brainstorm. Hancock immediately agreed. He wanted Detective Sherry White in the loop, particularly since it was her initiative that brought them into the case in the first place.

"What have we got?" Hancock asked as he and his partner sat down with Sherry and Charlie. They were using Sherry's office for convenience. "Let's make a list of what we think are the killers characteristics," Joe said.

Seeing an opening in the conversation, Charlie said, "First, I think that he is a traveling man of some sort, perhaps a manufacturer's rep. Second, he must be good-looking to charm all these beautiful women, and with a line of bullshit a mile long. Third, he's obviously a good golfer with money if he's using that particular expensive ball. Less skilled golfers usually play cheaper balls. Of course, he could have stolen the balls, or had free access to them. Lots of companies try to impress their executives and good customers by giving high-end balls as perks. He might travel for work and combine a sales job with a little extracurricular love making, rape or whatever floats his boat. He is obviously a psychotic SOB who thrives on having power over women. It could be someone who works at a golf pro shop and makes off with balls from inventory or members' bags."

"Charlie, that's a pretty good list," Hancock said. "It might be any of those or even someone who sells golf balls for a distributor or manufacturer.

"Also, you may not have noticed but these three murders all took place on a Monday night. That in itself is unusual and might have some meaning. Another key clue might be the number on the balls. The number 77 is on all the balls, so they had to come from the same batch. I understand that If someone special orders a dozen or more, then all the balls can come with the same requested number. Most hackers don't give a damn what the number is on a ball. A good player who's the superstitious type might want a certain number for good luck or he might play in tournaments and use the number to differentiate his ball from what others are using."

Sherry piped up and said, "Unfortunately, my gut tells me that we are going to see more of this. Until we do, or some other consistency shows up that gives us another clue, nothing will get us closer to a solution."

Agent Hancock spoke with authority and said, "I want to make sure that when that unfortunate thing happens again, which I have no doubt will occur soon, I want to be in a position to take immediate and effective action. I'm going to have the FBI notify every police force across the country, asking that we be alerted as soon as any similar murders happen."

"Great idea," Sherry said.

"I agree, because this guy is on the move and may never come back to the same place twice in one year, so we've got to be ready," Charlie said.

Joe's partner Paul Clark, who had been listening closely to the conversation, said, "Okay, we agree that bad things will probably have to happen before forward progress can be made. I wish I knew a little more about golf so that I could figure out the significance of the choice of golf balls. Doesn't the number 77 have something to do with luck in casinos?"

Hancock was unsure but responded, "I think it is a symbol of luck of some kind, maybe to do with angels or the roll of dice, but I don't really know. We have to look into that."

Sherry agreed. "Maybe the guy is a gambler," she said. "I have a friend in Vegas who's a dealer. He might shed some light on the subject. I'll call him later today."

"Good idea, Sherry," Hancock said. "Let's meet again in a few days if we have any new thoughts."

4

February 20, 2018

Agent Hancock got a call at his office outside Los Angeles about 9:00 AM on Tuesday. It was 12:00 PM on the East coast. The call came from James O'Leary, a detective in West Palm Beach, Florida. "How can I help you, Detective O'Leary?" Joe asked

"Agent Hancock, a few days ago our office got an alert from the Bureau with your name as the contact. It pertained to the possibility of someone taking advantage of attractive, young, working-age women, having sex with them, and then killing them in an unusual way. Unfortunately, we have just had a murder similar to your description right here in West Palm Beach. The woman was discovered in her hotel room less than an hour ago. No injuries that we could see, nothing disturbed. But the unusual thing was the way she died."

"Let me guess, James. Someone forced two golf balls into her throat and suffocated her. Does that sound pretty close to correct?"

"That is exactly what happened! How did you know?"

"We've been worried we would get a call like this, Detective. It's happened three times already on the West coast in just the same way."

"What would you suggest we do right now?" O'Leary asked.

"I want you and your men to check out the bars in West Palm Beach. Show the bartenders a picture you might have of the girl, and ask them and the waitresses if they had seen the woman with a blond guy about her age on Monday night. In the meantime, I'll contact the Palm Beach County FBI field office and make sure a special agent gets in touch with you before the day is out."

"Will do, Agent Hancock. We'll get working on this and wait to see your agent."

"Thanks for contacting us, Detective. Good luck finding this character.

"Oh, one last thing. Do you happen to know what type of golf ball was used to kill the victim?"

"Yes, it was a Medallist Tour ZX, the same ball I use when I'm feeling flush. When you lose those babies in a pond or palmetto bushes, it gets expensive. Oh, and the balls had the number 77 on them."

"Talk to you soon," Joe said, thinking about the growing complexities of solving this case.

Joe phoned Harry Knight, the FBI Agent In Charge of the Palm Beach County field office, and filled him in completely. Harry said he would have his best man contact Detective O'Leary immediately and would follow up on the case personally. Harry said he wanted to think about the case and would get back in touch when and if he came up with a useful idea.

It didn't take long. First thing the next morning, Joe's phone rang. It was 9:00 AM on the East coast, 6:00 AM in the West, and Harry Knight was calling.

"I'm sorry it's so early but I just got an idea that needs to be followed up on right now," Harry said. "I'm an avid golfer, like a lot of people here in Florida. I follow the golf tours and the players and watch lots of golf on TV. I was thinking about the dates when the three murders took place on the West coast, and realized that professional golf tour events were being held at approximately the same locations and on the same exact weeks that the murders occurred. For instance, the first killing happened in Indio, which is a city close to the tournament site in La Quinta, California.

"The next tournament was in Scottsdale at the Tournament Players Club course. The actual competition started on January 31, three days after the Mary Chapman murder.

"The next event was at Riviera Country Club in the Palisades area, right next door to the Brentwood neighborhood where there was a murder at the Ramada Hotel.

"And now we have a murder in West Palm Beach, three days before the start of the Honda Classic here in Palm Beach Gardens. There's gotta be some connection between all this. I don't know what it is, but if I have another brainstorm you'll be the first to know. One thing for sure, these are not random deaths. That's it for now, and I'm sorry I woke you up so early." Joe thanked Harry for his analysis and help.

Over the next hour, Joe and his partner discussed what Harry had laid out and had to agree

Harry's conclusions made sense. Joe called Harry Knight back in Florida two hours later. His call was put through immediately. "Harry, it's the opinion of our group here in California that you're onto something. The killer may have a reason to be on the East Coast for a few more months because this is high season in Florida for golf. You seem to have a knowledgeable background in golf, which could play a role in the case. What I'm suggesting is that it might be appropriate for you to take charge of the whole case. Of course, we will remain interested and willing to help in any way, should you need us."

"OK, I think that is logical," Harry said. "I'll jump right on it but will definitely keep you in the loop."

Agent Hancock had made a good decision. Harry Knight was a dynamic guy. He didn't let grass grow under his feet, he was a clear thinker and a good leader. The fact that he was engrossed in the game of golf could be a big help too if this case involved golf or golfers.

What Hancock didn't know was that when Harry was younger, he was one of the best young golfers in South Florida. His goal had been to try to get his PGA Tour players card, once he finished college. He started playing in satellite tour events and soon realized the depth of talent in the crop of players he attempted to play against. Disappointed, he gave up his dream and decided to find a real job. He felt that going into the armed services for a stint was probably a worthwhile idea. His time spent as an MP led him to apply to the FBI, where he quickly rose through the ranks. While Harry was in the military he was offered an opportunity to learn to fly as a private pilot, his longtime fantasy and passion. Through the years he continued flying, and obtained his instrument rating.

Earning his instrument rating was challenging. It required 40 hours of specialized flight training time, which was expensive. Learning to fly without reference to anything but the instruments is a demanding skill, requiring knowledge of the rules and procedures. It is a rating only a small percentage of private pilots ever acquire. But Harry knew that if he was going to travel to play in golf competitions or use an airplane for special FBI situations, he'd better be able to fly in times with less than perfect weather conditions.

Rather than dragging this required training out over a year, Harry chose the option of completing the training with an instructor in 10 compressed days. Doing this took a large chunk out of his vacation time, but he was happy because he accomplished his goal.

Once certified, Harry decided to buy a reasonably priced airplane which was equipped with the appropriate technology for all-weather flying. After an extended search, he found and bought a 1979 Cessna 182 Skylane in "great condition." It had a Garmin 530 GPS navigation unit that linked to an autopilot and good radios. Now he was ready to fly his Cessna 182 to regional senior amateur golf tournaments and, when necessary and permitted by the Bureau, to FBI work situations.

Harry was intrigued by this murder case, perhaps more than any he had been involved with for years. He knew the first step was arranging for a few other agents to follow up any leads they could find in the West Palm Beach area where the victim might have met the killer. There was a chance someone would recognize the victim or someone who fit the description of the California man seen in the bar in Indio, but Harry knew it was a long shot.

Early Thursday afternoon Harry asked his three most experienced agents from the Bureau's field office to meet with him for a strategy session. He opened the meeting with a full update on the series of murders and the facts about the cases. "Folks, I want us to just freewheel on this case," he said. "Don't hold back on any 'off the wall' idea you might have. This is what we at the FBI sometimes call a 'Pig's Wings Case,' one that is bizarre and strange.

"Right now, I'd like to hammer out a theory that seems logical to me, but I may be way off base. My theory is that the killer is somehow connected with people who are moving around the country, either as a part of, or servicing the needs of, the huge moving feast called the PGA Tour.

"We need to understand the scope of all this. It's not just the players who are crossing the country with their caddies. There are also equipment and ball suppliers, the club fitting vans, reporters, marketers, coaches and trainers doing the same thing. Moving vans are taking all sorts of gear from one place to another, including television and transmission equipment. And that's only part of it.

"But for the moment, let's focus on these few groups. The one consistent clue we have seen in every murder is the Medallist Tour golf ball. For you non-golfers, let me explain. The tour players themselves play about a half dozen different brands of quality balls. One ball in particular has, for the last few years, dominated the ranks of the players—the Medallist Tour ball.

"This ball comes in two varieties, each with slightly different spin characteristics. There's the Tour Z and the Tour ZX. With these murders, the balls used were all the ZX balls. This could help narrow down our search, especially if we're looking at the possibility that a player might have gone off the rails mentally.

"But let me say right now, I seriously doubt that any established golfer is the murderer. Our plan here is to eliminate people and groups from the suspect list, and to tighten the search as soon as possible. I think investigating the golfers might be the easiest and most logical place to start.

"Most players on tour are given balls of their choice every week by the ball manufacturers, more balls than they can probably use in that time frame. So there are likely lots of balls around of each type and these are accessible to a lot of people, including family members and friends. In addition, there are dozens of people, other than golfers, who travel with the Tour and are probably decent amateur golfers themselves who might use the same quality balls used by the players.

"You can see we have to cast a very wide net if we hope to find this guy before he goes to work on his next victim. This guy's MO could be to go to some town or city near a tour stop where he is unlikely to be recognized or bump into someone he knows. He meets a girl, romances her with plausible crap, and somehow gets her to register for a hotel or motel room in her name.

"Then he does his deal and leaves to go back to his job, probably somehow involved with the tournament as service provider, vendor or whatever, never to be seen again. It seems sick but not unbelievable. Do you guys have questions or thoughts?"

"Yes, Harry," Ted Gilpatric, a big, burly, no-nonsense guy sitting in the back row, said. "Where are we going to start with this? Who's going to focus on what? Your theory sounds workable, but it could become a maze with no exit point."

Harry said, "As I mentioned, Ted, I think it's highly unlikely that any player is involved. But I think we have to eliminate that possibility first and figure out an alternative path."

A bookish looking fellow named Jim Ellis sitting next to Gilpatric said, "Isn't there a tournament taking place this week over at Palm Beach Gardens?"

Harry responded, "You're right, Jim, and I think we shouldn't waste any more time. We've got to scope out the whole scene while we have a chance. Today is the first day of actual play at the Honda Classic, so the course and the surroundings will be a madhouse.

"I want to personally get the facts from the manufacturer about which golfers are playing the ZX ball, and that could be upwards of 50 or more guys. You people should go watch the event and get a feel for the flow of things and the people involved, like the vendors and such. There will be three more days after today, so we can talk about specific ideas later.

"Let's get going right now. I'll get you passes when we get on site. Split up and explore on your own, and we'll talk first thing tomorrow morning. Parking is at a premium so we'll all go in one car."

5

When they arrived at PGA National Golf Club, they pulled into a space directed to by security. Madhouse was an understatement. Tens of thousands of people milled around trying to watch their favorite players. There were small crowds following relatively unknown players and large groups watching the stars.

Harry suggested that the team just wander around following their noses and to also observe the scenes off the course, especially where the back-stage and vending action occur. Wearing suits and ties, the agents explored. They looked a bit different from the crowd of patrons who were sporting Izod shirts and Vineyard Vine shorts. Most people probably assumed they were with Security.

Harry went to see the golf shaft and grip experts in the Medallist Company service van. He introduced himself to the person in charge at the moment and asked, "Would you be able to tell me approximately how many of the players are using your company's golf balls in the event?"

"Well, not at this exact minute because some guys change balls occasionally. But we probably have about 100 or more of our balls being used today."

"How many would be using the Tour ZX ball?"

"Maybe 40 percent," he said.

"Would it be possible for you to get me a list of the players who use the ZX ball?"

"I'd have to ask my boss if I can give out that information. Why do you want to know that?"

"I can't really say at this point, except that this information might help solve a crime that is of great interest to us. Anything you tell me would be in total confidence."

"Okay. Give me your card and I'll ask my boss to get in touch with you."

Having gotten the ball rolling, so to speak, Harry decided to take a few moments to visit the practice range and watch the players who were working on their games.

He couldn't help but think back in time to the years he worked his ass off trying to become one of these highly skilled professionals. He practiced for weeks on end, and got to the point where he thought he might have a chance of making it on the Tour. But bringing good ball-striking from the practice tee to an actual tournament, where a player has to make a competitive score, is something he never accomplished well enough or often enough.

Golf and the PGA Tour have become unique in the world of sports for developing an environment that attracts and maintains a high level of honesty, civility and competitiveness among its players. There are relatively few problem people involved with the game. The fact that Harry was a golfer himself made him uncomfortable even investigating a situation like this.

The organization's strong management had found subtle ways to deal effectively with any issue that developed that could cast a bad light on the Tour.

But it's a fact of life, as with all large groups, that sometimes there are people who are not emotionally stable. They have been able to hide their deranged nature so that even folks who know them well cannot recognize their sick side. Harry's responsibility was to make sure he didn't overlook one of those people who might be living a double life.

When play had finished for the day, the agents made their way to the car to head back to the office and then home. Their experience had been eye-opening to all of them, except for Harry, who had seen it all before. They were surprised by the large number of workers, volunteers and staff that is required to host one of these events, as well as the countless press people milling around. There had to be hundreds of people making their way from event to event. Could the killer be one of them? Because of the unique schedule of the golf events and the timing of the murders, Harry became convinced that someone in that group had to be the murderer.

When Harry got back to the office, he had an idea and felt the need to check it out before he left for dinner. His thought was to find the results of the various pro tournaments that had been held so far this year, and ascertain who played and who didn't each week. If he could crosscheck that information with the list of players using the ZX ball, he could narrow things down a bunch. He badly needed that ball list!

The next morning, he got a call from the company that produces and markets the ball the FBI was focused on. The list they agreed to provide showed all the players who use specific versions of their golf balls. The company then uses these names for promotional purposes. They want the public to know all the great players who have chosen their ball. The company's only concern was that the list not be utilized in any negative way. Harry assured them that wouldn't be the case, and they faxed him the list.

Harry pulled out the result sheets he had assembled the night before and laid them out on the conference table. Then he took the list he had just received of the ZX ball users and checked to see how many of those had played in the tournament at La Quinta on January 25. There were 48 in that group.

Then he did the same thing for the tournament played on February 1, at the TPC in Scottsdale. There were 54 on that list.

Harry eliminated the name of any player who had not played both event. This moved the target number down to 42.

Doing the same cross-check with the list of players who teed it up at Riviera Country Club in Palisades, he eliminated nine more players who did not qualify for or who chose not to play that event.

He followed the same routine for the Honda Classic, currently underway at PGA National, and found many changes in the list because it was a World Championship event for which many lower status players weren't qualified. This reduced his up-to-date list to 22 players who had played in all of the earlier and current events and who played with the Medallist Tour ZX golf ball. This became his target group.

Harry was pleased with what he had accomplished with his theory, but knew that the group was still too large to productively investigate. He would have to think about his next step.

6

At 9:30 AM Harry got his team together once again to review his findings and hear any thoughts they might have. The agents were impressed that Harry had reduced the list to such a manageable number.

"Ok, guys," Harry said. "This is what I propose. I want to go through this list, which I think is still too large, and make a personal judgement call to limit the group further. That's because there are many pro golfers who are well known to anybody who follows golf and even to the casual TV golf watcher. These are people who have been vetted in a million ways by their fan bases and the press. Because they would be physically recognized in whatever town or city they went to, no one at this level of success would ever expose himself to a career-ending situation like this. Many of the players' caddies are also famous and quickly recognized because of TV exposure.

"By my calculation, and this is just seat of the pants stuff, I would say after going over the list, I found at least 12 of them who are particularly well known and should be dropped from our list. I want you to run background checks on the remaining ten. All the standard stuff. Maybe something will turn up, or not. Personally, I hope nothing does but let's find out."

By mid-morning the reports started coming in on those ten players. These remaining guys were not totally obscure. In fact, Harry had noticed many of them creeping up the leaderboards of various events over the past year. However, unlike Harry, the occasional golfer who isn't engrossed in the scores and goings-on in the world of golf would probably not know who they were.

Of the ten men, seven had absolutely clean records. Harry said he could, if needed later, make a few calls to his buddies to get a fix on these players, just to be sure. The unique drawing power of Southeast Florida, with its many golf courses and all the competitive opportunities in the area, has encouraged a large number of tour players, famous and unknown, to make their residences along the coast within 50 miles of Palm Beach. Finding dirt on a player's lifestyle was not going to be difficult.

Three men on the list presented Harry with bigger questions. Two had bad driving records involving DUIs. One had been caught using pot and was arrested. Two of these young guys seemed like they might be clean-cut, regular guys, and unlikely suspects.

The third man reportedly had some personality issues. He kept to himself more than most and was sullen and distant to the other players. Despite being a handsome blond guy with a competent golf game, he wasn't particularly friendly with other tour guys or the caddies. Nobody seemed to know if he had gone to seek help with whatever issues he might have.

"What do you think, guys?" Harry asked his small group who were now dressed in casual attire so they didn't stand out among the crowd at the golf course. Jim Ellis, who had commented before, suggested, "I think we should split up again today. Each of us should observe one of these three guys to see if anything weird jumps out. One of us should try to get a fix on other stuff happening at the event in case we missed something that could help. I'm willing to do that job and leave the golfers to you guys."

Gilpatric, the burly agent, said, "I understand that some players will be cut after today's play, so this may be our last chance to take a good look at some of these guys. They might be gone tomorrow and be out of our sight for a long time, maybe forever."

"That's it, let's get going and take two vehicles," Harry said.

When they got to the course, Harry said, "I would like to personally take a long look at this third guy we talked about. His name is Keith Bennett. In a general way he fits the vague description of 28 to 34 years old and blond hair. Of course, a bunch of guys fit that description. Keith grew up in the Florida Panhandle in a small country town near Panama City. I might want to follow him after play is over to see where he goes and what he does with himself. You guys split up, whichever way you decide. We'll touch base first thing in the morning."

Keith Bennett had a 1:32 PM tee time off the 10th tee. With half an hour to kill before Keith played, Harry walked over to the range to see if he might be there hitting balls. He was on the far left side of the teeing area, at least six hitting slots from the nearest other player. His caddy was with him, but he was standing quite a bit further from him than most caddies normally do. Harry's immediate reaction was that Keith and his caddy didn't get along very well. Keith was hitting the ball with a high draw and seemed to be able to hit towering shots and low cuts at will. "Nothing wrong with this guy's golf swing, but can he putt?" Harry thought, slightly amused, because the same question could be asked of most tour players.

When Keith decided to head for the 10th tee, he had to walk by at least a dozen players who were practicing. He never looked at one of them or said a word to them or to the fans watching from the large five-tier viewing stand.

In the first round Keith had shot a disappointing 74, which put him at risk of not making the cut. He had started the year doing quite well, but in recent weeks his game seemed to have fallen off. Harry sensed that Keith and his caddy were just going through the motions and not communicating with one another. Not a good sign. He was playing with two men who were also in the mid-tier of tour player status. These guys are always at risk of losing their "card" if they fail to keep their games at a high level. That could mean dropping back to what is now called the Web.com Tour, until they could fight their way back to the major tour by playing very well against a lot of hot shot young guys (many of whom have proven that they can play to the high standard of the big tour).

Keith played well at first, but on the 6th hole he pulled his second shot into a creek to the left of the green. From then on things fell apart. His relationship with his caddy seemed to be coming further apart as well. They started talking and pointing at each other in an exasperated manner. Keith ended up shooting another 74, two shots higher than the projected cut line.

While Keith was hanging around the score board waiting to see where the cut line would be, Harry Knight decided to have a casual conversation with him. He approached Keith near the score board and said, "I was following you for a while today. You have a very good golf swing and hit a lot of great shots. I'm sorry about that shot on the 6th hole that went into the creek. It seemed to get things going badly for you."

"Yeah, well thank you," he said with a disgusted look on his face. "I had a bad distance estimate and was given the wrong club, but I should have figured it out myself and not relied on someone else."

Harry said, "I noticed that things didn't seem very happy out there between you and your caddy."

"Well, it's hard to find someone who works smoothly with you. I had a great guy who was with me for three years, but he got sick and I had to make a go of it with this man. He was a player himself but couldn't make the grade. I think it still gnaws at him. Anyhow, that's the way it goes. I just need to rely on myself and shouldn't blame anyone else."

"It looks like you might not make the cut. How does that make you feel?"

"That's the way it goes with golf, you never know what the next week will bring so you have to forget it, mind your own business and move on. I plan to play the next tournament in Palm Harbor on the Florida west coast and hope to do better."

When he finished his conversation with Keith, Harry had a better feeling about the guy. He was still not sure why he wasn't liked by the other players. He told his field agents later in the day when they all gathered, "In my opinion this is not the man we are looking for so let's look elsewhere. How did it go with the two players you guys followed?" They both had the same feeling. "We couldn't see anything about these men that raised any concern," Gilpatric said. "They played great, seemed to get along with the others in their groups and are not in our opinion the murdering type."

"By the way," Harry said, "I made contact again with the ball manufacturer regarding any special orders of balls by the players with the number 77 printed on them. I'm hoping to hear back from them soon. Unless they give us a positive hit on the ball number, let's forget about the players themselves and eliminate them as suspects. My feeling is that they are not involved in any way."

7

Palm Harbor is a small city not far from the Tampa/Clearwater area, and a regular stop for the golf tour. When Detective Adam Grant received an alert Tuesday morning that there was a "big problem" at the Sunrise Inn in Clearwater, he drove over with his partner and arrived at the facility within 15 minutes. On the second floor of the motel, the maid had discovered a woman laying naked on the floor next to the TV cabinet. She was obviously dead and had been for hours. The bed was a mess and the woman's clothes were thrown around the room. It looked like there must have been some sort of a struggle.

When Detective Grant looked closely at the woman, without touching her, he spotted a weird thing. There was at least one golf ball in the woman's open mouth. Having read about a similar death the week before in Palm Beach County, he called the

FBI field office in Palm Beach which he discovered had been brought into the case. He asked to talk to the Special Agent in Charge and was put straight through to Harry Knight.

"Hello, Agent Knight, this is Detective Adam Grant from Clearwater. It looks like we have joined the list of cities that have become the target of the sick bastard who is raping and suffocating young woman in hotel rooms."

After hearing Adam's story, Harry said, "It sure sounds like the same MO from start to finish. Did the girl book the room herself?"

"Yes, she came in about 9:30 PM and seemed to be alone, according to the desk clerk. There are no obvious clues that I can see. The assailant must have taken great pains not to leave any prints. I don't think we have found any DNA evidence yet, but the team is still checking."

"Ok," Harry said, somewhat frustrated. "We've sort of hit a wall at the moment in our investigation. The theory we're working with seemed logical at first but it needs to be given a second look. Keep in touch if anything turns up that you think might help. In the meantime, we'll get back to you if we need your help chasing things down. I would ask that you check the bars and social haunts around

Clearwater to see if anyone can recall having seen her last night, alone or with someone. We're on the lookout for a blond guy around 28 to 34 years old who hangs around bars. But that describes a lot of guys in Florida."

"Sure will, and good luck with the search," Detective Grant said.

When the FBI team met that afternoon there was a high degree of skepticism about the effectiveness of the theory and system they had been using to eliminate possible suspects, along with obvious frustration with the results so far.

Harry said, "I think we should change our approach. What we've been working with concerning the players just isn't yielding anything, and I'm beginning to believe it won't."

One of the smartest guys in the group, John Cavanaugh, a younger deep-thinking guy, commented, "While lying in bed last night, it occurred to me that the system we have used still might make sense. But what we never considered is that each player is really a team of two people, himself and his caddy. So the system of elimination we have been using can apply to the caddies as well because they obviously go where the player goes. Plus, they have access to the player's excess golf balls. Maybe we should go back to the ten players we ran the backgrounds on and take a look at their caddies to see if there is a prospect there."

Harry said, "John, you are absolutely correct. Many of these guys are former players themselves and have access to any amount of balls from their player's bags. In addition, lots of them are good looking athletic men who could easily pass for a pro golfer. Could one of them be posing as a player and sucking in a gullible girl to a fake romance? It's absolutely possible. Let's run full reports on all ten. We'll have to contact the Tour offices to see if the contact information is available."

Harry thought he might be able to get a jump-start on the information by taking an immediate flight in his Cessna to the Palm Harbor area. Once there he might be able to actually lay eyes on the caddies

in question. They should be close to finishing the practice rounds for the Valspar event and preparing for the first round on Thursday morning.

Harry, without assistance, pulled his plane out of the hanger at the North Palm Beach County Airport and made the one-hour flight, landing at the municipally owned Clearwater Air Park. He tied down his plane on the ramp and made an online request for an Uber car for the short trip to the Innisbrook Golf Resort, the site of the tournament and a short distance north of Tampa.

When he walked toward the clubhouse, he bumped into Keith Bennett whom he had met the week before at PGA National. Bennett was coming from the 18th hole and didn't seem happy with the state of his game. But he seemed pleased to see Harry again. Harry hadn't revealed to him before that he was an FBI agent. Now he thought it was appropriate to do so. When he told him that he was looking for some general information and had come over from the Palm Beach office to investigate a few things, Keith didn't seem bothered in any way. Harry thought that was a confirming sign of his innocence.

Keith stated that he was ready for a break to do some extra work on his wedge game and putting, and wouldn't be playing the next three weeks. One of those weeks featured the Masters tournament which he hadn't qualified for anyway. He also said in a hushed voice, "I'm dumping my caddy after this event. I need someone with a new attitude around me."

Before leaving Keith, Harry handed him a list and asked if he knew the names of the caddies that these ten particular players use. He asked the question in a casual, non-threatening tone. Keith did know almost all the names, or at least the names they used. Harry thought this was a good start, and tomorrow, as the last practice round got underway, he would get a chance to actually see them working.

By the next afternoon, Harry had physically seen all the caddies he was interested in. Of the ten, four were too old to be possible subjects, two were completely bald and paunchy, leaving four prospective caddy suspects.

Harry tried to spend as much time as he could watching each one of the four, but soon concluded that there was no real way to assess their temperament while they were working and engrossed in their jobs.

One of them had the wrong hair color, not being blond. Of course, the assailant could have been wearing a wig. Then again, the team had been working with the assumption that the blond guy seen with the victim back in Indio was the murderer, which might be totally wrong.

Later in the afternoon Harry took a taxi back to the Air Park and made the relaxing one-hour flight over the pasture lands of South Florida and across Lake Okeechobee, towards the North Palm Beach County Airport, a general aviation airport which was Harry's home base. It was a time when he could be by himself to think and plan his next move.

8

On Thursday morning, Harry reported the progress he had made at the tournament site and gave his team the names of the four caddies who he thought could be the primary suspects, along with Keith Bennett's caddy. "So now let's talk about the timeline and some other things I have wanted to mention.

"Many of the players arrive at a new tournament site late Sunday night or early Monday so they can get a feel for the greens and work on the weaker parts of their games, or the specific shots that might be required at the new venue. Most of them would play in the Tuesday or Wednesday Pro-Am as an extra practice round. The caddies would have arrived before or with their players at the tournament site. They have a lot of preparation work for the event, including checking out possible new pin positions, assessing green speeds and the distances to obstacles, such as water or bunkers. Everything the pro golfer will want to know. Monday night can often be a free night for a caddy to take care of personal business or go out with his buddies.

"Every murder in this string has taken place on a Monday night, three days before the start of actual tournament play, which usually goes from Thursday thru Sunday.

"The next two events are the Arnold Palmer tournament at Bay Hill in Orlando, and then the Houston Open in Texas. The first one could give us the last good chance to test our theory and check on these four caddies because all four will be working the Bay Hill tournament.

"The Masters tournament starts two weeks after that. None of the players who use these four caddies have been invited to play there. So let's hope that we can settle this thing before then," Harry said.

John Cavanaugh, the young FBI agent whose specialty is criminal profiling, asked, "Depending on how the reports come back on the four caddies, do you think we ought to go to Orlando, say next Monday, and each of us watch one caddy the whole day and find out what he does that night? It will be our only opportunity to do that here in Florida before the tour goes west to Texas."

"I agree. Regardless of the reports, we should do that anyway," Gilpatric said.

"Okay," Harry responded. "It's our last shot, so Monday morning we'll go to Orlando. In the meantime, we should be getting the reports on these guys over the weekend."

Late Saturday afternoon Harry was notified that most of the information had been received and would be delivered to him within the hour.

The names of the caddies were Frank Slaughter, Richard (Icky) Brown, Joe Barrows and Charles (Ziggy) Ziegler. They were definitely a mixed bag.

Frank was the one who, physically, most resembled the man seen at the bar with the first victim. But the reports on him made him the least likely on paper. He had attended a Bible college in Tennessee and was a close friend and former college roommate of his player. He was a good golfer himself and hoped to play the tour one day. His credit history was excellent with a credit score of 760. He was also unmarried with no children.

Icky Brown was a typical drifter. He never went to college and had no real plan for his life. He had a son out of wedlock, who he sees occasionally. Not a bad criminal record, but he had been picked up on minor pot charges twice. Never in jail. He probably lives hand to mouth. Yet surprisingly he has stuck with caddying for three years and is respected in his trade. He's good looking, six-foot-plus with a quick smile and brown hair.

Joe Barrows appeared to be a jovial, regular and open guy who is considered a charming rogue. Has family in North Carolina, divorced with no kids. A competent caddy, but jumps around between players more often than most. His credit score is in the tank, probably from mismanagement as opposed to lack of funds. Six-foot-two, slightly overweight, blond hair and ready smile.

Ziggy Ziegler is a quiet, 33-year-old journeyman caddy. A professional who has been at the same job for eight years with the same player. He sticks to himself and has few close friends in the caddy group. He has a West Virginia background but little else is known except that his father and mother are dead. As an 18-year-old, he was involved with an abuse case but never prosecuted. A drunk driving conviction three years ago resulted in significant points on his driving license. He lives in the Jacksonville area of Florida, is slender, six-foot tall with sandy blond hair at near shoulder length, often pulled into a ponytail.

Harry Knight's team of agents left their Palm Beach County office at 8 AM Monday for the three-hour car trip to Orlando and the Arnold Palmer Bay Hill Classic tournament site. Once again, they were dressed casually and had a change of clothes ready, should they need to change for the evening surveillance. During the trip, Harry filled them in on the brief report summaries he had received.

The real focus of the team was not the daytime activities of the individual caddies. They obviously would be with their players, either on the practice range or at the short game area. Many golfers would be playing practice rounds, hoping to get a feel for the speed of the greens and the hardness of the surface for their approach shots. The caddies would be right there with them tending to their chores.

What was of interest would be what happened in the evening. Where did they go and who did they spend time with? The agents split up, knowing what their responsibilities were, and they agreed to meet or at least communicate with the team at 9:00 PM.

For the most part it turned out to be a fairly dull day for the agents. None but Harry were golfers. There was lots of standing around watching the caddies and players hitting balls and putting. The enjoyable part was seeing the celebrity players they had heard about, including Tiger, Phil Mickelson, Ricky Fowler and dozens of others they had seen on TV. Some of these super-stars relished the attention of the horde of reporters and Golf Channel analysts and commentators. Others preferred being by themselves, off in a corner of the extensive practice area.

When the day ended, and their preparation work was finished, many of the other caddies wondered off to relax or go to dinner with their pals or players. Some left individually, possibly with personal business to take care of or family members to call. Other guys hung around the club to shoot the bull or have a beer or two.

Ziggy and Frank stayed around the club and grabbed sandwiches to go with their beers. An hour or so later they left separately and went to their rooms. That was a normal thing and no surprise to the agents.

Another caddie, Icky Brown, headed off to the local Ruby Tuesday with a friend and was back in his room before 7:30, watching television.

The fourth man, Joe Barrows, stopped at Chick-Fil-A and then went to a movie theater to see "Dunkirk."

In all, it was an absolute dead-end and wasted day. Harry thought, so much for the system! Granted, it was only an attempt to narrow the focus of the investigation but it had not been productive in any way. The good news was that nobody got murdered at the Arnold Palmer event in Orlando. Of course, Keith Bennett's caddy wasn't around this tournament.

When Harry checked his email late in the day he found a message from the Medallist ball manufacturer saying that their records indicated no player had ever ordered Tour ZX balls with the number 77 printed on them.

Discouragement settled on the agents like a morning fog.

9

On the way back to Palm Beach that evening, nobody did much talking. Even Harry Knight, sitting in the back seat with Jim Ellis, seemed lost in his thoughts. When they drove past the Yeehaw Junction exit on the Florida Turnpike heading south, they knew that they were about half-way home. John Cavanaugh, sitting in the front passenger seat while Ted Gilpatric drove, turned around and said to Jim Ellis, "Jim, the day last week when we were in Palm Harbor at the Valspar event, you spent most of the day looking at the operational aspects of the event and the vendors and equipment marketers. Did you see anything that piqued your interest, or did you talk to anyone in sales or product marketing that had followed the tour across the country?"

"Well," Jim said, trying to recall his activities that day, "all the action off the course was set up in a very organized way and seemed to be run professionally.

I didn't get into detailed conversations with many people because they were straight-out taking care of the many patrons crowding around.

"But I did have one interesting conversation with a guy from Los Angeles when I was hanging around the practice putting green. This fellow, I think his name was Bud Willis, was a club pro somewhere near Los Angeles for a few years. But he lost his job for some reason. He'd been hired by a small company owned by an older man who had invented a putting training device that he had patented. It was called 'Quiet Hands'.

"It was designed to help train a golfer to maintain a stable left wrist when putting," Bud had explained. "The owner needed someone for a couple of months to go to the Tour events and introduce his product to the touring pros, hoping also that amateurs would see it being used and start buying the product."

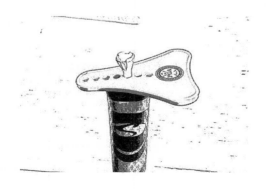

"So this sales guy said that he started going to the tournaments in the Southwest region, sometime in the middle of January, beginning with Southern California. He came east when the tour moved into Florida. Bud said he would probably work the job until just before the Masters. He had to have permission from the Tour to approach the players and could only do it Monday and Tuesday during the practice periods. He gave me his card. He was a handsome guy about 35 or 40, nicely dressed and well spoken. That's just about the only long conversation I had with anyone," Jim said.

"Did you detect any kind of BS factor about him?" Harry asked.

"No, not really, he was pretty smooth though," Jim said.

"Ok, Jim, here's what I want you to do. Since you have his business card which has the name of the company on it, contact the owner without alerting the salesperson, and find out everything you can about the guy's history. And John, you run a full report on the guy first thing in the morning."

The next afternoon, Jim Ellis knocked on Harry's office door and walked in with a slight smile on his face. He had just talked to the owner of the putting trainer company and had gotten a few nuggets that might bear fruit. "According to the owner, this Bud guy was a good golfer but not good enough to make it on the tour. He stayed in the golf business as an assistant pro. He was fortunate to be in the right place at the right time and got hired to be Head Pro at a small club called Highland View in California.

"I guess he couldn't control his libido and tried to make it with a few members' wives. That didn't go over big and he was bounced in less than a year. Of course, the word gets around pretty fast in golf circles, and he couldn't even get an assistant's job in the area. He was desperate.

"Then he heard that the 'Quiet Hands' inventor was looking for someone in sales and he went to him begging for the job. The 76-year-old owner didn't plan on keeping anyone in the job long term, so the guy's history wasn't important to him. Bud looked the part, knew golf, and he could talk on the same level as the tour players. That was good enough, according to the owner."

When the background check they requested arrived at the office the next morning, the story got even more interesting. John Cavanaugh said, "The truth is that Bud Willis was actually accused of attempted rape by one of the woman he tried to snooker into an affair. Then the woman decided she just wanted to bury the thing when it came time to press charges. I guess she wasn't guiltless and hadn't discouraged the guy soon enough. But the Board at the club got Bud out of there without delay.

"The other thing that turned up was that Bud Willis is in a bad way financially. His credit report is a disaster. It makes me wonder—could this horny guy be on the prowl for a rich lonely widow to save his ass?"

"Wow," Agent Knight said. "We may be on to something here. My guess is that he can't do any more business this week with the pros at Bay Hill because the actual tournament starts tomorrow and today is Pro-Am day. He may already be moving to his next and last tournament site in Houston."

"I'm disappointed to have to say this," Harry said. "We have worked this situation hard and maybe have come up with our man, but unfortunately we are too far away from Houston to be effective. I'm going to get back to Agent Joe Hancock in Los Angeles and return the case to him to hopefully finish the deal. Anyway, this Bud Willis guy is not coming back east because his job will be finished after the Houston Open next week."

Joe Hancock was delighted to get a call from Harry Knight who he had not heard from for a few weeks. He wasn't happy, however, to find out that the nightmare case was coming back his way. "Harry, are you sure this guy's the murdering bastard?"

"There's no way to guarantee that, Joe. We've eliminated all the tour players from our list as possible suspects and all the caddies but one, and he is probably a dead-end also. The organizations that service the tour are all high-grade companies. There is no way to check on all the coaches and trainers who work with the players, so if it isn't this guy in Houston, we are back in the fog again.

"By the way, some of us think there is a possibility that this sales guy, Bud Willis, may be trying to hook up with a rich divorcee or widow to ease his financial problems, and who knows, maybe even a marriage. His home is in the Los Angeles area."

"Thanks, Harry. We'll be looking at this character and hope you've found the right target. At least the guy may be more focused on finding someone to solve his financial situation than on knocking off some young secretary or sales woman for the sick thrill of it. I'll keep you in the loop."

Harry said, "You should know that he is allowed to do his sales demonstrations with the pros only on Monday or Tuesday, so it's most likely he might be going back to Los Angeles after that."

10

Agent Hancock sat down with his partner, Paul Clark, to explain everything he'd been told by Harry Knight. They reviewed their notes and realized that Detective Ben Angle had reported to them that a bartender from the Nightfall Grill in Indio had actually talked to the victim. Apparently she was with a "good-looking guy at the bar" the night she died.

"We've got to get a photo of this Bud Willis so we can show it to the bartender to see if Willis is the same person who was at the bar that night. If you fly down to Houston and can get a photo of the guy while he's working his sales job at the Houston Open on Monday of next week, we might get a leg up on this thing. We can't wait until he returns to Los Angeles because we don't know where he lives or might be going next."

"Makes sense to me," Paul said. "I'd be happy to go to the tournament. I might even get a chance to see Phil Mickelson, one of my favorite players."

Paul was in his early 40s, with a ready smile and good instincts. He was the perfect man for this job.

Paul landed in Houston and, after getting a rental car from Avis, made his way to the Golf Club of Houston in Humble, Texas, a few miles from Houston. He thought to himself, "I've heard this tournament is one great show and I can't wait to see it." The venue, the field of world class golfers and the enthusiastic golf crazy fans in the Houston area make this a special treat for the patrons every year.

Paul didn't get a chance to attend many events like this and he loved golf, even though he was a self-declared hacker. Hopefully, he could find this Bud Willis person early, take his picture and have some of the day left to watch players hit balls on the range. He might even get to follow Phil or Jordan Spieth during their practice rounds.

When he arrived at the golf course, he went directly to the huge practice putting green near the clubhouse and started searching for Bud. It was difficult to pick him out from the professional players because he was about the same age as many of them and looked like a player. When he was unable to see anyone who he thought might be Bud, he went to the large practice tee area a few hundred feet away.

As he walked along with the moving crowd he saw a smaller, more private putting green where five or six players were working on their putting stokes. On the furthest side of the green, an attractive man was chatting with one of the pros. The man was, temporarily, placing a small unique device on the end of the player's putter grip and demonstrating how it worked. This had to be the right guy!

Paul had a non-threatening manner, yet he knew he had to be careful approaching the possible suspect. He walked slowly over to the pro who Bud was talking to and said, "I'm a fan and wonder if you'd mind if I took your picture while you work on your putting?" The young player smiled and said, "Okay, go ahead." He was obviously pleased to have Paul's attention. When Bud started to move out of the way, Paul quickly asked, "Please don't move. I would like to show you working together as you were before, rather than just posing."

Bud said, "Sure, no problem."

Paul snapped a few photographs he thought could do the job. "Thanks very much for the pictures, guys. Have a great tournament." Now he could watch some golf. It was another five hours before his flight home.

The next morning Paul found his best photo of Bud, transferred it to his computer and cropped it to enlarge Bud's face. He had one good face-on view that would work. He emailed the photo to Detective Ben Angle in Indio along with a tag telling Ben that, "This is the picture of a possible suspect." He asked him if he would chase down the bartender to see if he could recognize the man in the picture from the night in January when Amanda Joyal was killed.

At 4 PM, a call came in from Indio for Agent Hancock. It was Ben Angle. He told Paul that the bartender was off for the day but he had found him at his condo pool catching some rays. The man had no doubt the picture was of the same guy he talked to that night at the Nightfall Grill in Indio. Bingo!

Early Wednesday morning, Agent Hancock moved to put the clamp on Bud, to get him into custody and off the street. Other than the photo confirmation, there was no absolute proof that he had killed the women. They did, however, have the timeline evidence that would prove he had been in or near all the locations where women had died on both the West and East coasts. They needed to interrogate this guy soon. His next call was to the Bureau's Agent in Charge in the Houston area. He asked him to send someone to the Houston Open site to locate and pick up the suspect without delay.

A team of four FBI field agents were immediately sent to find Bud and take him into custody. They took copies of the photographs Paul had snapped the day before.

By the time the team got to the tournament site, Bud Willis was nowhere to be seen or found. According to several pros and a bar manager, he had been around the golf course for four or five days, having arrived from Florida on the past Friday, but had apparently finished doing his demonstrations of "Quiet Hands" and then left for good.

As a courtesy, Joe Hancock called Harry Knight later in the afternoon to keep him up to date on what had happened in Houston. Harry had a brainstorm. "Joe, I'll contact the ball manufacturer again to see if they have any records of a George (Bud) Willis having special ordered any Medallist Tour ZX balls, number 77, in the past year. That would give us all the proof we need. I'll be back to you as soon as I get any word about the balls.

"By the way, it seems to me that this is a critical time in this entire case because Bud is finished working his job after this week and will soon be pursuing any possible way to survive financially. Keeping track of him is going to be a total crapshoot."

11

Alice Campbell was a looker. She was also a well-known, 37-year-old amateur golfer from Houston who couldn't stay away from the exciting activity taking place around the golf tournament. When she bumped into Bud at the clubhouse bar, the chemistry was intense and immediate. They hooked up enthusiastically.

She had been divorced for four months from her physician husband, a workaholic and a non-golfer. They had no children, so lifestyle complications didn't exist for her.

Having helped her husband financially by working while he went to medical school, her divorce settlement arrangement was substantial. The fact that her husband held a significant position at the MD Anderson Medical and Cancer Center didn't hurt her settlement either.

After spending three nights together, the conversation between Alice and Bud turned to the idea of going away together for a week or more. The fact that Alice had a property in the Cabo San Lucas region of the Baja Peninsula in Mexico made their decision easy. Bud tried to play it cool but his excitement level was rising just contemplating the possibilities of this relationship.

Even though he didn't look it, Bud was getting older and was staring 40 in the face. It was time for him to rethink his future and how he lived his life. He began to realize that the macabre thrill he had gotten by killing the last girl in Clearwater was not as exciting as during his earlier escapades. He wasn't sure why.

After meeting Alice, he began thinking more about his financial survival than just satisfying his sex drive or pursuing the thrill of killing his targets. The question in his mind was, could he set aside or resist his tendencies toward doing damage to young women or was it beyond his control? He knew that if he continued on the same track, he would eventually be discovered and his life would be ruined forever.

Perhaps this trip was a test for him. Bud was seriously ready for a change in his lifestyle and the freedom from needing to work to survive. He had often heard the phrase, "One can fall in love with a rich person just as easily as a poor one," and that sounded like a plan to him.

Whether Alice was the right one for him or not, she had all the attributes he needed, with her significant resources and desire to have an agreeable companion and lover.

He had read books about people with split personalities, like Jekyll and Hyde, and how it was seemingly impossible to treat these people effectively. Perhaps he fell into that category. Maybe he couldn't be treated or cured of his affliction, but he could try and restrain himself. Having a wife and a nice life might give him the reason he needed.

Direct flights from Houston were plentiful and cheap. Within three hours of Bud's last putting demonstration on Tuesday, the two lovebirds were winging their way to Mexico, completely oblivious to the search going on for him in Houston.

They played golf every day on a challenging Nicklaus-designed seaside course, snorkeled in the reef just yards from their villa and soon became satisfied lovers. Bud was beginning to think he had a future he'd only dreamed about. There he was, in an oceanfront villa with a gorgeous gal paying the bills, his financial pressures off, at least temporarily. "The hell with California, this place is a paradise," he said to himself.

Bud was sitting on the terrace of their small but elegant villa which looked southeast over the shimmering water of the bay. His imagination was working overtime. He asked, "Alice, are you happy?"

"Of course I am, Bud. This trip has been a blast. In fact, I've always liked being here, but with you around it's been extra special."

"Then why not stay longer?"

"We could, maybe for a few more weeks. But I have a large home and numerous social and other obligations back in Houston, so it's not that easy. We could go back and forth a bit, if things work out between us."

"Okay. In the meantime, let's enjoy it and see how things go," Bud said with a smile of satisfaction. Yes indeed! Things looked promising.

The FBI team in Houston, which had agreed to help Joe Hancock's group capture Bud Willis, thought they had done all the right things. Their first mission was to try to locate someone around the Houston golf course who might know Bud Willis or his whereabouts. They met a few players who had talked golf business with him for brief periods, and some waitresses and a bartender at the club who remembered seeing him around the place a few days earlier, but none had any specific knowledge of him or knew what he was doing in Houston.

The bartender was the only one who had any information at all. He had seen Bud talking and laughing with a woman named Alice Campbell, who he knew to be a Houston resident and an active golfer. They had been in the restaurant together for several meals and ordered drinks from his bar.

A rundown on Alice Campbell turned up basic information but revealed nothing negative about her or her family. An attempt to contact her at home had failed, so they left a message. Eventually they discovered that there was a group of women she played golf with regularly, one of whom, Mary

Higgins, was a close friend. Mary revealed that Alice had recently met a nice man "who she enjoyed spending time with." That was all she knew.

When the agents asked Mary where she thought Alice might have gone, she mentioned that Alice and her ex-husband had owned a villa or condo in Mexico. She wasn't sure where but she knew Alice liked going there because of the excellent golf courses.

The next inquiry was to the airlines that served Mexico's popular resort areas. The first airline they talked to, United, had a record of a flight taken by two people to San Jose Del Cabo on Tuesday afternoon at 2:30. The flights were booked in the name of Alice Campbell and paid for by a credit card in her name. They had purchased round-trip tickets with return flights the following Tuesday.

Someone with a badge would definitely be waiting to greet the pair when they returned to Houston.

The following Tuesday, an FBI team was prepared to confront Alice and her new friend at the gate. Four special agents — a woman named Sara Bendix and three men — were ready to place Bud under immediate arrest. They positioned themselves directly at the departure ramp. There was no way for Bud and Alice to escape and two men were in the background ready to close in should Bud try to make a run for it

Unfortunately, when Alice and the suspect failed to disembark from the airplane, the team had to regroup and deal with a situation which was now beyond their control. The two questions were: why didn't they return and when would they come back?

One new piece of the puzzle convinced the FBI that they had the right guy in their sights. Harry Knight reported to Joe Hancock that the golf ball manufacturer had confirmed to him that George Willis had ordered two dozen Medallist Tour balls in December of last year, of the exact variety and identification number used to kill the women across the country. Now they just had to catch him.

12

Special Agent Tom Burns of Houston was having coffee with the team of field agents involved with this case and expressed his major concern. "If this character is the guy who killed those five women over the last eight weeks, it wouldn't take much for him to do it once again to Alice, particularly in a foreign country with nobody watching him."

"That's for damn sure," agent Frank Mendoza said. "But if he was having financial troubles, why would he kill the goose with the golden eggs?"

"Unless he could talk her into a marriage first and end up with some of her money," said Sara Bendix, a thoughtful and valuable member of the team.

Hearing this, Tom thought about how they could move this investigation to a more productive track. They had no idea when, or even if, the two lovers would be returning to Houston. The thought occurred to him that perhaps there was a way to save Alice from being killed and get their hands on the suspect at the same time.

The plan formulating in his mind was sending an undercover team to Cabo and then to somehow get Alice alone where they could talk to her about her tenuous situation. They could hopefully get her cooperation in bringing Bud back to Houston.

He thought Sara Bendix and Frank Mendoza might be the best agents to go undercover because they both spoke fluent Spanish. They would need to find out where Alice lived and get a clandestine message to her, all without tipping off Bud.

This was an unusual operation that involved gathering information in a foreign country and making contact with an American citizen that could be considered outside the rules for the FBI.

Approval for this would be needed by Martin Lopez, the Special Agent in Charge, who headed up the Houston Bureau. Martin was reluctant at first to adopt this strategy, but finally concurred.

The following day, Sara and Frank, posing as tourists, left on a United flight to San Jose Del Cabo.

The peninsula was bathed in glorious sunshine and overflowing with pink hydrangeas and purple irises when they arrived. The smell of the sea hovered over the small historic village of San Jose Del Cabo. Neither Sara nor Frank had ever had the time or extra money to explore the Baja region before, so this would be the most memorable work trip of the decade for them.

The question now was: where did Alice live?

They knew it had to be somewhere along the 32-mile stretch from San Jose Del Cabo south to Cabo San Lucas. Route One, the road between these two towns, clings to the seacoast at a distance that not only provides magnificent elevated views of the bay to the East, but also allows room for multiple high-end developments on both sides of the road. The area was certainly being developed fast but as yet had not been ruined. Golf courses flourish in many locations and have become a major tourist draw.

There was no easy way to know where Alice Campbell might have acquired a home in the area. She and Bud could be anywhere between the two towns or in one of dozens of small planned communities, probably near one of the golf courses. The villa or condo might not be owned in Alice's personal name, so luck would have to play a big role in locating them.

Sara suggested that they start on the South end of the area, in Cabo San Lucas, and try to find a government taxing authority office where they could look up Alice's name and address.

But they had no luck finding any reference to Alice or her former husband, in spite of a very helpful tax department head. The Señora was just happy to talk to Americans who were so fluent in her language.

The pair enjoyed a delicious lunch of camarones and tacos along with tasty margaritas at a cozy cantina a few blocks from the busy tourist hub. The town itself was charming, but the spectacular outcroppings a short distance off the beach stole the show. Sara considered shopping for family gifts before she left town but there was no time today. She was determined to return alone someday.

Driving back north to San Jose, they passed the Cabo Real Golf Course on their left, and stopped to inquire if the management recognized the name "Alice Campbell." The club had excellent records of golfers who had played recently, but no one with Alice's name showed up on the starting tee sheets.

There were five or more golf courses they could check out, should they not find Alice soon.

Suddenly they remembered that someone on the FBI team had mentioned that Alice and her husband might have taken title to the property in a different name, such as a LLC or a trust. The only way to determine that would be for an agent in Houston to contact Alice's ex-husband. Frank called his office and requested that information, hoping that someone in Houston would follow up soon. Meanwhile, Frank and Sara waited anxiously for that crucial title information.

When they got back to the town of San Jose, they inquired at the local tax office and ended up with the same results as in Cabo San Lucas. There was no record of Alice Campbell.

It was about 3:00 in the afternoon and Sara and Frank had run out of ideas, except perhaps to visit those other golf courses.

A fine golf course called Club Campestre was within a short ride from San Jose, and they decided to take a chance and inquire there. It was a magnificent facility set high in the rolling terrain and adorned with flower gardens, lush fairways and wide panoramas of the ocean. It was a superb place for rich Americans who loved golf.

Frank went to the desk and asked if some friends they were looking for, "Mrs. Alice Campbell and a guest," might have registered to play the course during their visit to the area.

"As a matter of fact, yes," the receptionist said. "Actually, Mrs. Campbell and her friend are out on the course right now and probably have only a few holes remaining in their round. If you want to wait for them, you are welcome to sit on the veranda."

"Thank you, Senorita, but please don't say anything to them when they come in as we will want to surprise them at their home when they finish playing."

"Very well, have a nice day," she said.

Sara and Frank found a safe spot where they could observe Alice and Bud finish their round without being noticed. The descriptions of the two lovers the FBI office had obtained were accurate. They made a most attractive couple.

After Bud and Alice finished their round, they stopped at the clubhouse, ordered ice tea and lemonade, and went to the veranda where they sat at a colorful umbrella table. The view looking across the sloping hills and valleys of the golf course and out to the sparkling sea was breath-taking.

Bud said to Alice, "Your game was very good today. You seem to be improving more every time we go out. I think you scored around 90 today, which is nothing to be ashamed of on an unfamiliar course like this one."

"Well, Bud, it might have something to do with playing with you and watching you hit those great high iron shots. That's one thing I can't seem to do. I'm always worried about getting the ball off the ground and topping it when I use my longer irons and hybrids."

"I noticed that," Bud said. "But I didn't want to butt in when you had such a good score going. If you don't mind, I have a little suggestion that might help."

"Sure, okay with me," Alice responded. "I always want to improve, so don't hold back."

"Ok, I think it may be as simple as you being more aggressive about hitting down on the ball. You should know that fairway clubs are designed to hit down on the ball, and to even take a divot. Hitting down actually makes the ball go higher. Doing that will also compress the ball more and give you a better ball flight and extra distance. Many amateurs try to lift the ball into the air or pick it cleanly off the grass which is self-defeating and leads to bad shots."

"I've heard that before but have never actually tried to do it," Alice said. "Now I will, and thank you."

"By the way Bud, I noticed that all the balls that you have in your bag have the number 77 printed on them. What's the story on that?" Alice asked.

"Oh, many years ago I read something about 77 being a lucky number so I started writing the number on my golf balls as an identification. Later, I found out that I could order them that way from the manufacturer, so I do that now. It's probably silly, but I am a little superstitious about numbers."

"Whatever floats your boat," Alice said. "Let's go home for a swim."

When the golfers got in their car to leave, Frank and Sara followed from a safe distance behind.

Their journey was only a couple of miles, ending at a charming hibiscus and rose-covered villa on a cliff perilously close to the sea, # 4244 Cabo Place.

The agents had solved the first problem and they both felt relieved to have at least started things moving. Now came the hard part.

They had booked two nights, in separate rooms, at a quaint small inn in San Jose and were able to walk to a sidewalk cafe down the dappled and heavily shaded main street. Over dinner they plotted the next step.

They needed to be creative. Somehow, they had to find a way to get a secret message to Alice. Their note had to convey they wanted to meet her alone, and most importantly, that the meeting was serious business and must be kept secret from her friend.

They decided that Sara should deliver the message so Alice would be less likely to be scared off, should they accidentally come face to face.

The next morning Frank parked their rental car a few hundred feet away from Alice's villa, hoping to see when and where they might go for the day. In less than an hour Alice and Bud opened the garage door, took out their bikes and rode into town for breakfast.

The agents followed them and parked as far away as possible, yet close enough to keep them in view. When Alice and Bud left the cafe, almost an hour later, Bud seemed to gesture that he would ride back home ahead of Alice, perhaps to give her the time she wanted for personal shopping.

Sara realized that the time was right to deliver the note. She walked towards the cafe, keeping her eye focussed on Alice's every movement. When Alice stepped into a small boutique, Sara walked by Alice's bicycle and placed a note in her basket.

The note said, "We need to talk soon. Your life may be in danger. Come to the cafe tomorrow morning about 9:00, alone. Don't tell your friend or anyone. Friends from Houston."

Alice saw the note when she pulled her bike out of the rack, read it and started looking around. She thought, "What does this mean? Why am I in danger? Should I be worried about Bud?" She was a nervous wreck.

She couldn't stop herself from walking around the main street of the village, trying to see who might have left her such a note. Nothing unusual caught her attention. Everything around her seemed like normal tourist activity. A few younger couples were looking in store windows, giggling and holding hands, probably honeymooners enjoying the sights. One middle-aged couple was having coffee at an outdoor cafe. It couldn't have been these people, she thought.

Sara and Frank were pleased that the note had been received and the message read. Now it was up to Alice to gather enough courage to meet them, whoever they were.

13

The bike ride back to her house on Cabo Place was 20 long minutes of absolute hell. She was scared. She didn't know what to think or how to act in front of Bud. If the warning was about him, then acting strange might cause Bud to start asking questions. What puzzled her most was the part in the note about her life "being in danger." She wondered, "Do these people know what they are talking about? Could it be some kind of a scam? Should I be afraid of Bud?"

She finally made the decision to do what the note said, primarily because it directed her to meet at the Cafe in San Jose which is a place she knew well and where she felt safe. She had no choice but to act normally around Bud, even if that included having sex.

When she arrived at the villa, Bud was out on the terrace sipping a rum punch, which was also her favorite drink. She tried to act happy and said with a flirtatious smile, "Well lover, I hope you saved a little of that for me."

Bud said, "Of course. I've made a pitcherful and expect you to catch up to me before too long so we can have a little afternoon delight." She had no choice but to play the part.

Later in the afternoon, Bud asked about her shopping. She told him that she was focused on a colorful linen sheath dress she had seen at the boutique, and that she planned to go back to try it on and perhaps have it altered tomorrow morning.

"Want me to come along and give you any advice?" Bud asked with a smile.

Alice said, "No, that's not necessary, and besides, I have more shopping I want to do. Just get a good book and sit by the pool. I will be back in no time."

She hardly slept during the night, tossing and turning with worry.

At 8 AM she dressed in casual clothes and took the car out of the garage. She then went back into the house to get a straw sun hat she had forgotten. Bud was drinking his coffee and catching up on the news when she came up behind him and kissed his head. "Ok, I'm going now, see you in about an hour or so," she said.

"Have a good time, dear," he said.

Alice found a parking spot within 50 feet of the cafe. She then breathed deeply and gathered herself for what was ahead. It was a tension-filled moment.

Half a dozen customers sat at tables in the small cafe which primarily served baked goods and coffee. The only table occupied by more than one person was way in the left rear, just before the kitchen. A well-dressed couple in their early 40's was having coffee and muffins. When she looked at them, the woman got up and gestured to Alice to join them at their table. As Alice approached, Sara Bendix put out her hand and introduced herself. Then she turned towards Frank Mendoza and introduced him as well.

"Please sit down, Alice, and thank you for coming after seeing our note. Frank and I are FBI Special Agents from Houston. We have no jurisdiction or authority here in Mexico but we do have two very important missions."

Sara said, "First, we believe that your friend, Mr. George (Bud) Willis, is the perpetrator of at least five murders of young women in various cities in the States. We don't have sufficient proof at this point to prosecute him, but what we have is enough to take him into custody when he returns to the US.

"Secondly, and more importantly, we are concerned for your safety while staying with this man. He has killed in the past, without any reason that we know of, and we believe he would do so again. It is possible that because you have substantial assets he desperately needs, it would be a reason for him to take advantage of you financially, which might be temporarily keeping you alive.

"We know this is shocking and undoubtably worrisome to you, but we have a plan we need to discuss. Would you be willing to talk to us about this?"

"My God, this is unbelievable," Alice said, trying to keep her voice down. "It can't be true. He is a very nice man who seems caring and considerate. This can't be an act."

"We assure you, Mrs. Campbell, that our superiors in Houston would not have us fly to Mexico and make contact with you without the threat being real. You can't take the chance that we're wrong."

"You probably have a point there. But what can I possibly do?"

"Here's what needs to happen, and very soon. You must think up a reason why you have to return to Houston, immediately. Make it good so it sounds believable. Bud would obviously go back with you. We will remain here until you fly out, and we will be on the same plane with you. We will avoid talking to you so Bud won't get suspicious. If he buys the deal, he will be in taken into custody when you land and you will be safe. Until then, we will have to wait for a message from you telling us which flight and when you are going to leave.

"You'll have to be natural about the way you act and try to remain as relaxed as possible. If he thinks everything is going well for him, you shouldn't be in any danger. If you feel you are in danger at any time, text us and we will help you, even if we have to blow our cover. Is that clear to you?"

"Yes, I understand, but I'm not the strongest person. I just hope that I can hold myself together. How do I reach you?"

"Here is our cell phone number. It's listed under Sara Bendix. You know how to text, don't you?"

"Yes, I do it all the time with my girlfriends."

"If you get desperate or worried and feel you need help, we are registered at the inn down the street as Mr. and Mrs. Frank Mendoza from Houston."

As they walked out of the cafe, Alice said goodbye to Frank and Sara with a handshake and a nod. She started towards her car, only to bump face to face into Bud. He had decided to ride his bike into town to surprise Alice. He looked at Sara and Frank, wondering who they were and why Alice was at the Cafe. As they started to walk away, Bud asked, "Do you know those people, Alice?"

"Well, no, I met them in the cafe. They just arrived yesterday from Houston for a visit and we had coffee together."

"What were their names?"

Alice said, "I think they said it was Mr. and Mrs. Mendoza." She prayed her "lack of memory" was convincing.

"Did you get the dress you wanted?" Bud asked.

"No, I decided to grab some coffee first and got tied up chatting with those nice folks. It was thoughtful of you to come and surprise me, Bud. I'll be home soon."

Alice walked immediately to the boutique and selected a dress she hardly needed. Then she bought tonic and rum at a small market and headed back to the villa.

If she could pull it off for one more day, she would be on a plane out of here and safely home in Houston.

14

Arriving at her house, she spotted Bud in the pool doing laps. She tried her best to look normal and natural despite a rapid heartbeat. She found it difficult to look him in the eye. Smiling was easier.

"Did you have a nice chat with your new friends from Houston, Alice?"

"Sure, they were pleasant, but that's it. They are not friends. You know, a lot of people from home come to Cabo because of the cheap direct flights. Why do you ask?"

"No reason, I was just wondering if you knew them from Houston."

"As I told you earlier, I had never seen them before," Alice said.

She had been racking her brain to come up with a story that would be plausible and believable about why she needed to return to Houston right away. Finally, something popped into her mind. It was tax return time! She called her accountant's office to ask if everything was okay with her tax return. She knew it was correct, but if Bud ever checked her phone, she wanted proof that she had made the recent call.

During a casual lunch of tuna sandwiches and lemonade, she said to Bud, "Dear, I hate to say this, but I called my accountant in Houston this morning to check on my tax return preparation which I had worked on last week. He discovered that I had left some things out by mistake and that need to be pulled together. There are forms I have to sign before next week's April 15 deadline. Since my divorce, the tax situation has gotten a little complicated for me. I never had to bother about it before. My husband took care of everything. But this means we have to go back by tomorrow, but only for a few days. I'm sorry," Alice said with a sad look.

"That's too bad, Alice. I thought we were having a great time and was looking forward to a few more weeks in paradise," Bud said.

"There's no reason we can't have just as much fun in Houston because I'm a member of a golf club there and a health club as well. It won't exactly be tough living. But maybe we can get in a last golf game here this afternoon?"

"Great, and how about a last swim in the bay?" Bud suggested.

As the day went on, Alice went through the motions, smiling and seemingly happy, but Bud detected a subtle change in her. "What was the problem?" he wondered. "Hopefully nothing."

Bud had always been the untrusting type with over-active instincts and he relied on them to guide his actions. He would have to see how things went for a short while, but he was getting funny feelings in his gut.

Alice made a reservation with United Airlines for a 10:30 AM flight back to Houston for two people the next morning. Later, she went into the bathroom and sent a text to Sara's number, saying simply, "United 10:30 AM".

Sara and Frank were proud of what Alice had done so far. It had to be frightening for her. Sara made their reservations for the same morning flight, hoping to get seats as far as possible from Alice and Bud.

Late that night, even after making love, Bud still had the lingering feeling that things had changed with Alice. She hardly looked in his eyes and seemed stiff, just going though polite motions. It still annoyed him somewhat that when he'd gone into San Jose to surprise Alice, and saw her with the people from Houston, that she made no effort to introduce him. They were only about ten feet away. It seemed out of character for her. And they sure didn't look much like tourists to him.

Very early the next morning, while Alice was doing laps in the pool, Bud went inside and looked at her phone which was sitting on the dining table. She had indeed called her accountant. But then he noticed a text sent to Sara Bendix about a United flight at 10:30 AM. He wondered, "What is that about? Who is Sara Bendix?"

Alice didn't have much packing to do for the trip home because they came from Houston with as little clothing as possible in carry-on bags.

They left the house about 9:00 AM and took their rental car to the airport. Bud dropped Alice off at the terminal door and returned to the rental car area.

As Bud drove around the corner of a small building used by the rental car company for check-ins and returns, he noticed the two people from Houston, Mr. and Mrs. Mendoza, walking towards the terminal, apparently having just returned their rental car.

"That's an odd coincidence," he thought. "Why would they be going back two days after flying down to Cabo? Tourists don't usually do that."

Bud was on the alert. When he went into the small terminal he saw Alice sitting in a waiting area alone. She had picked up the tickets and boarding passes from the check-in desk and was ready to board. Mr. and Mrs. Mendoza sat in another area on the opposite side of the room. There was no attempt made by either Alice or them to say hello or to communicate, even though they must have seen each other. It was just another strange minor thing that made Bud's instincts twitch.

When the 14 people waiting were instructed to board, the Mendozas jumped up and got in the front part of the boarding line. Bud, intentionally, hung to the rear so that he and Alice would be the last people to board. As they approached the ticket taker, and the beginning of the ramp, Bud said to Alice, "I have an intestinal issue that won't wait. You go on and board, and I'll be there before they close the doors." Alice boarded and sat in her seat, feeling safer every minute.

The crew got the plane completely buttoned up and ready for the final door closing and takeoff. Bud had still not boarded. The pilot insisted that they couldn't wait any longer and had to push back from the ramp. Alice didn't know what to do. Sara and Frank, sitting in the very back of the plane, were not able to stop the plane from its scheduled takeoff.

By this time, Bud was driving out of the airport property in the rental car he had not turned in. He started driving north without a clear destination but with a sense that he had escaped a trap and that his instincts had saved his bacon once again.

When the United flight landed in Houston, it was met by the FBI team who were anticipating taking Bud into custody. Sara and Frank told them what happened and expressed their embarrassment at losing the suspect. His action to avoid returning to Houston cemented their belief in his guilt even more.

Alice Campbell left the airport feeling exhausted and quite wiped out by the whole experience. However, she had a story to tell her golf group that would keep conversation going for months to come. She also felt like one lucky lady.

Alice was a rational woman who knew she had made the right decision in working with the

FBI. But deep down she was sad because she had enjoyed Bud's company more than she expected and had fantasies about the life they could lead together. It was so much fun to play golf with a male companion, a pleasure she could never have with her ex-husband who had no time for or interest in the game she loved.

The FBI talked to Alice, hoping to get a hint from her about where Bud might be heading. Alice told them that she was clueless about that and suggested that Bud seemed to have minimal knowledge about the Baja and Cabo area. "He could have gone south, but I really don't know," she told them.

The agents were realizing that Bud was a unique and slippery character who was going to be a challenge to find and capture.

15

Bud Willis had only a vague idea of the area to the north of the San Jose region. All he knew was that he was heading towards California and that the US border was about 1200 miles away. He assumed that there were towns along the way with accommodations of some sort.

He acquired a map at a fuel station that showed a town called Loreto, 300 miles to the north. It was a resort town of about 18,000 people, right on the eastern shore of the Baja peninsula with restaurants, hotels and lots of tourist attractions. A perfect place to disappear into and become invisible, should he ever have to do that.

The Loreto International Airport was also located there and featured flights to the States. If he wanted to go, he had a quick option available.

Bud settled in for a possible drive of five to six hours which was ideal as he would arrive in Loreto before cocktail time. He also knew that the town would have communications and available internet because it was a resort town.

The fuel gauge on the car indicated a nearly full tank. Even though the vehicle was well used, it was a newer model and seemed reliable, so he could relax and enjoy the trip without worrying too much about a breakdown.

Bud was sorry that the affair with Alice hadn't worked out. She could have been a great solution to his problems. He wondered for a few minutes if he had blown a good thing by going with his gut and not taking the flight to Houston. His father had always impressed upon him the "better safe than sorry" theory, and Bud had followed those words to the letter.

That, plus his quick instincts, had been why he had avoided any entanglements with the law as he pursued his relationships with woman over the last few years. His only screwup had been losing his job at the golf club because of that bitch in California he was hoping to have sex with.

Driving along, with time to think, he found himself contemplating the Jekyll and Hyde split personality issue again. Did that mental sickness describe him? The strange thing was that he could have a perfectly normal relationship with women and romance them and take them out to dinner, as any man might. He actually enjoyed their company. But when he went to bed with them and had sex, something changed inside his mind.

He became a different person. It was like he was a drug addict hooked on a substance he desperately needed. When he found himself in that situation, his mind only thought about the thrill of dominating and killing the woman he was with. He hadn't had that feeling for a while though, not since Palm Harbor.

When Bud drove into the center of Loreto, he was a little surprised by the lack of paved streets and the loose chickens and other animals walking around. Then the Gulf of California came into view. It offered the same sparkling water and unending vistas he had experienced in the Cabo region. The hotel that first caught his eye was the Villa del Palmar Beach Resort, right on the bay, with multiple pools, bars and probably luscious women.

Within an hour he had checked into his room, stripped off his traveling cloths and pulled on his swim trunks. First, he would have a dip in the large pool, then a rum punch, then an unknown evening adventure. Not a bad deal.

What he discovered about Loreto surprised him because he had never heard of the place before. A collection of islands right off the northern coast of town were begging to be explored. Many had blissful beaches and calm waters, ideal for paddle boarding, something Bud always enjoyed. There were secluded beachfront restaurants on the nearby mainland, perfect spots for getting to know some impressionable young lovely.

He could see himself spending a few extra nights or weeks in Loreto. It was peaceful and affordable, both of which he needed.

As he strolled around the extra-large pool deck, which had a swim-up bar and multiple young ladies sitting on slightly submerged stools watching him, he could feel his excitement grow. How lucky could he be?

16

Agent Tom Burns of Houston was feeling as stifled by the failed attempt to arrest Willis as he had been by any prior case. There was simply no clear place to turn. Bud might see the handwriting on the wall and stay in Mexico. On the other hand, there was no way for Bud to know he was even a suspect, so he might slowly work his way back to Los Angeles where he supposedly lived.

"We need to put the airlines on notice that Bud is a wanted man, and that we should be notified if he boards a plane heading to the States," Agent Burns said during a meeting in his Houston office with Agent Frank Mendoza. "It's unlikely that he would try to drive straight through the entire way to the border crossing into California at Tijuana. It's a 16-hour trek on lousy roads with few facilities."

"Maybe Willis would do it if he was desperate and knew someone was on to him, but he doesn't know that yet," Frank said. "I think we have to assume that the suspect will at some time in the near future go back to LA to at least collect his belongings or maybe move back in. We have to find out where he lives and keep a watch on the place, just in case he shows."

"You're right, Frank. I'll move on it right away and contact Joe Hancock in the LA Bureau and ask him to set up the search and take care of putting out the word on this guy.

"In fact, there is no chance that Bud would show up in the Houston area again so we might as well turn the case back to Hancock where it all began weeks ago," Tom said. He also felt a certain amount of relief for getting this case off his back.

Hancock could see the logic in turning the management of the case back to his office, but joked with Tom when he heard the news. "Well, I guess the Houston office just couldn't handle the job and had to give it back to somebody who could," he said.

To complete the circle, Joe ironically called Detective Sherry White of the Los Angeles police department, the officer who first contacted the FBI about the killings. He was lucky enough to catch her in her office. "Hi Sherry, it's Joe Hancock of the FBI, remember me?"

"Of course, I do, Joe. How's the case of the killer golf balls going?"

"That's why I'm calling. Can you believe this? We thought we finally had the guy cornered on a plane heading back from Mexico, but he skipped the flight and is now on the loose somewhere in Mexico or on his way back to LA. I'm calling to see if we could count on you guys to find out where he lives in LA and to put a bulletin out on him."

Joe continued, "Up to this point, we think that he has killed at least five women since this thing started in Indio back in January, using the same bizarre MO. We want to put this guy away before he goes on another killing spree."

Sherry called her partner, Charlie Broms, into her office to tell him the "good news" about getting the case back, which she said with a touch of sarcasm.

The easiest place to start was with the Department of Motor Vehicles which issues drivers licenses as well as auto registrations for the state of California. The process required a current address, but often people move and do not notify the department that they have done so.

Charlie checked out the address Bud had given. It was an apartment on Rosalind Street, but the owner of the building said that Mr. Willis had moved about seven months prior to an unknown address.

The US Postal Service did have a forwarding address for him, but it was for a postal box in his former neighborhood. The box was in a private mailbox store called Mail Monkey. They needed to check it out and keep tabs on the place.

Sherry and Charlie were having coffee at a Dunkin' Donut and brainstorming about what they were facing when Charlie said, "You know, Sherry, I don't think we are going to get any warning about Willis crossing the border. The FBI will certainly put Bud on a watch list for any airline he might try to use to get home, but I think he'll take his time and drive back though Tijuana.

"He undoubtedly has his passport and would have received a USA tourist visa when he and his girlfriend flew to Cabo. With these papers he might move easily through the border. It's doubtful that any boarder guard will even bother to check a list for a blond guy like him who looks like a US citizen. All he would have to do is fill out a simple form and pay $22.00 and he's in. According to Mexican rules, he can stay there for up to six months, so we might not see him for a while."

"I agree, Charlie," Sherry said. "It wouldn't be too hard for him to get through the border station. My guess is that he will likely stay in Mexico for a while to let things cool down. Why not? Except that he's driving around in a car the police are looking for.

"If he heads for the border I see him doing one of three things: leaving the Mexican rental car and crossing as a pedestrian, and then taking a bus back to LA; or renting a new car on the US side of the border; or just keeping his Mexican car, which is in his girlfriend's name, and driving it to LA and dumping it. I think he would want to avoid any additional paper work and would keep the Mexican car for a while."

"I agree with that," Charlie said. "It also might make it easier for us to find him and to keep track of him after he crosses the border, at least until he dumps the Mexican junker. Let's tell the FBI what we have concluded so that they can take whatever steps they think necessary. I'll contact Agent Hancock".

17

Loreto was a lucky choice for Bud. He loved the hotel, the beach and, in particular, the single women who thronged there. Each of three nights he had met someone who enjoyed his company and who was willing to participate in an evening of dancing and lovemaking. These ladies would be returning home before long and then be replaced by another group. What a deal!

He didn't want to mess up this good thing by engaging in his ultimate thrill. He was tempted, but he controlled himself to ensure he wasn't discovered.

He was aware of the six-month tourist limit for visits to Mexico but wouldn't want to stay that long anyway. It would soon get hotter than hell with temperatures above 100 degrees as the summer approached. Maybe he'd stay a few more weeks. He had a fresh credit card with a significant limit that would work just fine for that length of time, should he need to use it. However, he didn't plan on doing that.

The hotel had an internet service which he decided to use. He wanted to take a look at the news sites in Houston to see if any mention had been made about murder investigations of the dead women. He couldn't find anything from the news services about the subject. Finally he came across a video interview of Tom Burns, an FBI agent in Houston, done by a CNN reporter. The news gal, a fresh face on the network, asked a question about what the FBI was doing to chase down the guy who had killed all these women across the country. "Are they being forgotten? Are their families going to get justice?" she inquired.

Tom responded, "The FBI is doing everything it can to find the person. We have a photograph of the man which enabled us to identify him as the leading suspect, but he has escaped to a foreign country. We are sure the man will be found and brought to justice eventually."

"They must be talking about me," Bud thought to himself. "Where the hell did they ever get my photograph? Wait a minute, it must be that guy at the Houston Open by the putting green!"

Bud was jolted by this revelation. This changed everything. He now knew he had to be on his toes to make sure that every single step he took was carefully planned out. He realized that he had to go back to LA eventually, and the longer he waited, the more ways the FBI would figure out to trap him.

They obviously had no idea where he was now. They might think he went south to Cabo San Lucas, an active tourist mecca with lots of people and facilities to hide in. His only worry was that any credit card use might give away his location, so he decided to take off the first thing in the morning. One more night of pleasure!

In the meantime, Agent Hancock in LA decided to contact all the rental car companies in the San Jose section of the Baja that might have rented a vehicle to Alice Campbell about a week ago. A logical start was speaking with the largest company at the airport, and they reported that they had indeed rented Mrs. Campbell a red four-door 2014 Nissan. They gave the plate number to the agent. The car hadn't been returned as scheduled but was guaranteed by a valid credit card, so they weren't overly concerned about it.

However, when the company later found out that Mrs. Campbell had returned to Texas three or four days before, they did become concerned and said they would start checking on it. They assumed the car was down in Cabo San Lucas where there was a large airport, or maybe it could be up in the city of La Paz to the north of San Jose.

Meanwhile, Bud tossed and turned though the night, planning his trip across the border at Tijuana. The journey would be more than 900 miles through rough, sometimes mountainous terrain, and according to "Maps" on his iPhone, it would take about 15 hours. He had to make sure that he drove very carefully and not get stopped for speeding. He hoped that any police he might encounter wouldn't be looking for the license plate on the rental car.

The first thing the next morning, Bud got an idea. He went out to the parking lot and examined the cars that were parked there. Fortunately, the lot was somewhat remote from the hotel itself. His jackknife had a built-in screwdriver that he used to swap his plate for one on the rental car parked next to his. This solved one problem. So long as he didn't get stopped and have to show the registration, which would not match the new plate number 7652MK, he was okay.

After packing and wolfing down a quick breakfast, Bud got into his car and drove away. He didn't bother to stop at the desk to settle his bill. He only had a few hundred dollars in cash and didn't want to use his card. He tipped his hat to the gate man and said, "It's a great place, I'll write a rave review for Trip Advisor. Adios!"

Bud stopped at the first gas station he found, filled up and checked the oil and tires. Before leaving, he made a point of asking the station owner how long it would take to get to the town of La Paz to the South, the opposite direction he planned to go. "I'll be back in San Jose eventually to return the rental car, but I have heard great things about La Paz and want to check it out. Have a nice day!" he said.

His plan was to drive at least ten hours the first day, leaving about five or six hours the next. He calculated that he would be able to drive though the border crossing in late afternoon the following day, when many Americans would normally be returning to the States from a Tijuana shopping trip.

Around noontime, the maid at the Villa del Palma Resort realized that the guest in room 201 had left the hotel for good. When she reported this to the hotel desk, it didn't take them long to figure out that they had been duped by a con man.

They promptly put their security man on the case and his first inquiry was at the gas station close to the hotel. The attendant told them that the guest had stopped and filled up with fuel and then headed to the South. "He said he wanted to go to La Paz and on towards Cabo San Lucas," the attendant reported.

The desk manager immediately called the police in La Paz and San Jose del Cabo to alert them that an American man about six feet tall, blonde and driving a red Nissan was heading their way after skipping out on thousands of dollars of room charges.

18

The day after Bud drove north, heading for Tijuana, the man who had rented the automobile that sat next to his red Nissan in the parking lot, returned the car to the rental company. Of course, the paper work didn't mesh with the switched plate numbers on the car, and all hell broke loose.

Going on the previous information about where the suspect was heading, the hotel security and rental car company contacted the police to the South about the new plate numbers on the stolen rental car. It was now about noon.

When the original rental company in San Jose got wind of the notice regarding the change of license plates on their red Nissan, their concern turned to anger. They called the police to ask them to issue an all-points bulletin regarding the theft of their car. It was now 1 PM.

Bud stayed the first night in a seedy motel, one step down from a flea bag. But a bed was all he cared about after driving 11 brutal hours. After a quick cup of coffee, he left the motel at 8:00 the next morning and headed toward Tijuana, five hours away. During his trip he had to stop at two roadblocks, which he found out were quite common on Mexican roads. There were no problems either time with the *policia*, who barely checked his documents and let him pass.

His confidence level notched higher every hour he got closer to the border.

By 12:30 he was waiting in line, nudging slowly towards the inspection booth. At 1:00 he was showing his documents to the border agent, paying his $22 fee, and looking though the open gate to freedom in the US. They let him pass and he was gone.

Within two minutes, the all-points-bulletin came through to the border agents regarding the red Nissan with the stolen plate. They remembered the man whom they had let though the crossing just minutes before, and put the word out to the authorities, including the California Highway Patrol and the local police. Barely minutes later, Bud heard the wail of police sirens from a mile or so away. Bud felt fear spread though his body. His hands started to shake. "Shit! Could somebody have just realized they let a fugitive through the gate?" he thought. "No, there is no way it could have happened that fast," he said, trying to convince himself. But his anxiety increased.

Even though he thought they weren't after him, Bud followed his theory of "safety first" and drove into the first parking garage he could find. He took his bags and left the car in a spot on the third deck that hopefully might not be discovered for days.

Right around the corner stood a McDonalds, perfect for a quick lunch before moving on to somewhere safe. A Big Mac with fries did the trick.

Joe Hancock saw the notice come across his computer screen around 2:00 PM, indicating that an American being sought on charges of theft of services and of an automobile had just entered the States from Mexico. It piqued his interest. After checking with the border agent to get a description of the man, he became convinced this was their guy. Joe faxed the photo of Bud to the border agent who confirmed the identification. Joe then put out an all-points bulletin for the area that stretched from the Mexican border to Los Angeles.

By this time, Bud had hailed a cab to take him to the nearest bus station and was waiting comfortably in his seat for the trip to start. All he knew was that he would go to LA and figure things out from there. He had no idea that he had stirred up a hornet's nest.

Agent Hancock had a hunch that Los Angeles would be Bud's destination, so he called Detective Sherry White. "Hi Sherry, I don't know if you have read the notice that was sent out, but we may have our guy on the run. He somehow made it through the border before being arrested for stealing a Mexican car."

"Where do you think he is now?" Sherry asked.

"We don't know for sure but we are looking for the car. It's a red 2014 Nissan four-door with Mexican plates that he used to cross the border. We assume that he will drive it to some safe place and then dump it. We also think he might be heading your way, to Los Angeles. I suggest you tell your people to be on the lookout for a well-used, red Nissan car, plate number 7652MK. Also, if you have any fix on his residential location, maybe you can stake it out for the day."

"Thanks for the heads-up but we don't know where he lives. He left one apartment months ago and didn't give a forwarding address. We did find a postal box for him that we could check out, however," Sherry said.

"Hey, that's better than nothing. Give it a try."

"Will do, and thanks for the tip."

When Bud left his apartment on Rosalind Street months before, he rented a room for a year in a private home two blocks away. He kept his clothes, an extra golf bag and any papers he might need someday in his rented room. No one knew about his accommodations, and his landlady had no clue who he was, except for his name. He had prepaid in cash for the year and that is all the woman cared about. Since he was never there, it was easy money. That rented room was Bud's destination.

It was 4:00 in the afternoon when the police in the US border town finally started cruising through the in-town parking garages looking for the missing vehicle. On the third level, backed into a spot next to a large post, was a red Nissan, a junk of a car, dirty with mud. This was the vehicle they were looking for.

The local FBI agents developed a theory that the suspect had dumped the car not long after crossing the border. They figured that he might still be in the area or acquired another car somehow.

But then, he also could have taken the train or a bus wherever he was going, before the all-points bulletin had been issued. The best guess was that he was headed back to LA where he had lived and probably kept stuff he would want.

When Bud got to LA, he made his way to his rented room just before dark. He packed up everything worth having, including his extra golf equipment, and called a cab. When the taxi driver arrived, Bud told him that he would be making his way to the San Francisco area and was going to meet a friend who'd be giving him a ride. He said he wanted to go north about twenty miles outside of greater LA to meet this friend in Van Nuys. The cab driver was happy to get the profitable fare and told Bud he'd take him wherever he wanted to go. Bud's survival instincts were guiding him once again.

Sherry White and Charlie Broms had turned their entire attention to the search for Bud Willis. They checked all the bus and train stations in the area but came up empty. One of the bus terminal ticket agents thought he remembered seeing a guy of Bud's description getting off one of their buses around dinner time, but that was it. That information might mean he was still around. They had an officer stake out the Mail Monkey Store all day but no one looking like Bud showed up. Maybe he would pick his mail up the next day.

Agent Hancock contacted the credit card companies hoping get a hit on Bud's use of his credit cards. Fortunately for Bud, he had a large stash of cash hidden deep in his golf bag in the rented room, so he wouldn't need to use his credit cards, at least for a while.

When he got to Van Nuys, he saw a Holiday Inn Express and told the taxi driver he was meeting his friend there. The motel wasn't full, so he took a room for one night. It was well located and convenient to the bus and train stations. He was still trying to decide which transportation he would use in the morning. Luckily, breakfast was included with the room, so he didn't have to waste any time or money in the morning.

Bud had not firmly decided where he was going. He knew he was leaving LA for good. His life had taken a bad turn there, and he was not safe from the bloodhounds sniffing him down, trying to tighten a rope around his neck. He might even leave California. His prospect of employment in the golf business was dim, having been fired from his old club job. A bad reputation in the golf business was a killer, particularly with all the young assistant golf pros looking for a club position to keep their new careers alive.

He knew he would figure something out if he had enough time to study his alternatives. A peaceful train ride might be a good opportunity to do that.

The next morning, he boarded the 8 AM Coast Starlight train heading up though the Central Valley towards Redding, north of San Francisco. This special train featured sleepers and dining cars. Hopefully this would give him the opportunity and time to plot his future.

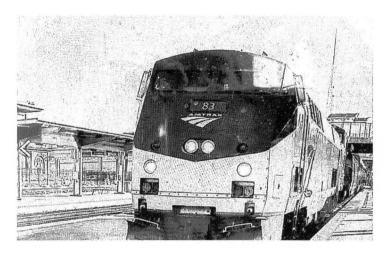

Taking the train was a little expensive for him, but considering he could avoid motels and restaurants, it would keep his exposure to a minimum. This train would also be an unlikely prospect for a police search since it's primarily a tourist excursion train.

The frustration at the Bureau was starting to take a toll on Joe Hancock. "This no-good bastard is beating us at every turn. He's always just ahead of us, whether it's the border crossing, the bus terminal or some train station. He's like a ghost. He is not using any credit cards, yet he is supposedly broke. How can he manage that?" Hancock asked.

His partner Paul Clark responded, "He may not be broke, just a deadbeat who lets his creditors suffer and doesn't give a damn. He's probably been squirreling money away for years."

"I don't see how we're ever going to catch him unless he uses a credit card or another young woman gets in his sick clutches and dies with the same MO, giving us a fix on his new location," Joe said. "And I sure as hell don't want that to happen."

Paul speculated, "Do you think he would try to leave California for a more remote area to the North?"

"It's hard to say," Joe said, racking his brain. "Maybe, but everywhere we've had any contact with him has been in a warm weather place. I doubt he would be heading for Canada or even Washington State, but who knows."

"We know he likes golf, but there are hundreds of places where he can find good golf courses and pick up some kind of work," Paul said.

Hancock's only real hope of locating Bud was if he used his credit card. Otherwise it would be tougher than finding the proverbial needle in a haystack. Bud had no phone, no bank account and no known location. Plus, California is a very big state. And he might not be in the state at all!

Sherry White had one possible card to play. She had placed an officer inside Mail Monkey with the hope he'd spot Willis if he showed up. She could only provide the stake-out for a few days at most, because she couldn't spare an officer with so many other important crimes around the city.

19

The first day on the train was an experience that Bud absolutely savored. The train brochure touted the spectacular scenery passengers would see of the redwoods, mountains and rushing rivers, and the hype was no exaggeration. He felt that if he had the money and the time, he would have taken the train all the way to Seattle. Perhaps he would do that someday. Right now he had a different agenda.

Bud regretted not getting a sleeping compartment. But in spite of sleeping lightly and turning a few times trying to get comfortable, he did get a decent night's sleep in the large lounge chairs.

During dinner in the dining car, Bud had met two couples from San Diego who were doing a west coast excursion all the way to Canada. They were planning a visit to the city of Victoria on Vancouver Island. Hearing their description of this Canadian city tempted Bud. Maybe that should be his destination. But what could he do there to make a living? He had saved only about $25,000 in cash, not much for a man on the run who needed a car.

Bud was more relaxed then he had been in years. He didn't reflect on his past often, but somehow this leisurely trip got him thinking about how he came to this place in his life. He knew he was a hated killer on the run and undoubtably thought of as a detestable human being.

He felt differently about himself. He had grown up in a life of privilege in Louisville, Kentucky. His father was a well-respected local physician and his mother was a stockbroker with a small investment company. When Bud was a young teenager, he didn't grow as fast as his classmates; that would come later. He had bad skin, was skinny with big ears, and was overall an unattractive package. He was ignored and shunned by female schoolmates.

Being a single child didn't help because he had no one to lean on who could help him feel better about himself. Bud became more resentful each year, which led to further rejection. He developed a deep-seated hatred of the hotshot, popular girls in his high school. They considered him worthless and wouldn't give him the time of day. Even after he had a growth spurt and outgrew his awkward appearance, he couldn't outgrow his sour attitude.

The only place where he was happy was on the golf course. That's where he could be himself. His parents joined the local country club when he was 12 and dropped him off there almost every day. He loved it. He picked up the game rapidly and became the best junior golfer in the club within a few years. It was all he wanted to do. Hitting balls, practicing his putting and playing in tournaments was his life. The best part was that he didn't have to deal with people who might not like him. His talent spoke for itself. He was at peace.

Then his parents were killed in a devastating car crash coming home from a charity dinner at the club. It ruined his life. He had to live with an aunt and uncle who weren't interested in taking on the burden of bringing up a young boy. The money that would have allowed him to keep playing golf dried up, and he felt helpless. He was able to go to the University of Kentucky on a golf scholarship and played on their golf team which was the only positive in his life. The lack of money and social skills kept him isolated from friends, but he made it through the U. of K. to graduation. And then, he only wanted to be a golf professional. A touring pro!

But it didn't work out because he just wasn't good enough to play on the big stage.

He thought his only path to success and any kind of happiness was to become a club professional. He bounced around for eight or nine years from club to club as an assistant pro, becoming more frustrated with each move. Finally, he was fired from his first Head Pro job over an incident with a woman at the club.

Bud thought that maybe he could make it in the golf business as a sales rep. At least he could travel and meet some people who didn't already know him. It was a chance to start over. But despite his handsome appearance, his ingrained dislike of woman and their high-maintenance ways drove him to find pleasure in his own special way: killing them.

Bud got off the train in Redding and took a cab to a used car dealer who had reasonably priced autos in decent condition. He found an older Jeep for a cash price he couldn't refuse. He was on the road within an hour, stopping first at an In-N-Out for a burger. He drove west on Route 3, then joined with Route 36 which took him to the coast. His plan was to head north on coastal Route 101 to the Oregon border and beyond to his destination. So long, California!

Spectacular was the only word to describe his route. The roads took him around bays, beaches and rivers, through small towns he had never heard of, past high cliffs and best of all, the fabled redwood forests in Prairie Creek State Park. He didn't stop overnight until he had crossed the Oregon border and arrived in the small town of Brookings. He found a motel with clean but modest rooms.

It was strange. Crossing the border bought him a surprising level of peace. "Who'd ever think to find me in this area where there are not many people or things to do?" he thought.

Before he left Brookings to head further north, Bud stopped at a Starbucks and stocked up on caffeine and baked goods. He was starting the most remote leg of his trip so far—nearly a hundred miles of forest, coastal inlets, unbelievable views and damn few people. It's all good, he said to himself.

20

While he was on the train the prior day, he had a chance to look at maps and magazines to get some ideas of where he might go and where he could, hopefully, find a job that didn't require him to give his Social Security number. Bud wanted a reasonable place to live but where he could still do the things he wanted, like play golf.

The most important thing was not being found by the FBI. It occurred to Bud that he would increase his chances of staying safely away from discovery and capture if he took on a new name. He chose Mike Simmons as his new handle.

Once he read about it, there was no question the place he found fit the bill. He had been driving on the coastal road for an hour and a half and his destination was only 20 miles away. His excitement grew. The town was small, right on the ocean, and had only 3300 residents. There were beaches, a river running through the tiny town, one restaurant, and a pub. The town was called Bandon. He liked the description of the place, but what really got his juices flowing was what existed a few miles away: The Bandon Dunes Golf Resort.

According to what Bud read in a golf magazine, "This is a world-famous place, highly regarded by avid golfers, that exemplifies the look and feel of Scottish and Irish links golf. There are four courses designed by the best of today's golf designers with high grade accommodations to match. Golfers fly to Oregon and drive to the resort, which is right on a magnificent stretch of the wild Oregon Coast, for two or three days of the most pleasurable golf in the United States."

This sounded like an isolated paradise to Bud. The fact that all players had to take caddies rather than golf carts meant that there could be lots of caddy work for an experienced golfer like him. He read everything he could get his hands on about the place, including that it was developed by a greeting card mogul named Mike Keiser who has a great love of golf and the environment. Keiser had made the commitment for the good of the sport. Bud had heard of this place before, but never paid much attention to the hype.

Bud gave serious thought to the relative safety of choosing Bandon Dunes. He knew it was a bucket-list destination for many golfers from all over the States, but its severe remoteness and the associated costs make it only a dream for other than well-off golfers, and not many of them knew him. The vast majority of police officers and FBI agents wouldn't even know the place existed. Furthermore, he would be one of many caddies working as independent contractors. The caddies are generally low profile types so he would fit right in. He felt comfortable about living away from the resort in the small town of Bandon.

When he arrived in town he went directly to the pub to ask about possible accommodations. He was told about a Bandon town resident who might be happy to have a long-term tenant for a small garage apartment he had fixed up. Bud introduced himself to his new landlord as Mike Simmons. It felt good. "Mike" had a sandwich at the local restaurant and then got himself dressed for a job interview at Bandon Dunes.

Pulling into the long driveway to the resort, he was stunned by how remote this place was. The owner was obviously a man of guts and vision to build even one golf course in a place as unpopulated as this, never mind four courses. "Mike" would later come to see the true beauty of Keiser's idea and concept.

Mike looked presentable. He knew golf and the caddy life, and he was ready to commit to a long-term job. The manager eyeballed him, chatted a bit and hired Bud on the spot. He could start work the next day.

Mike asked, "Can I walk around any of the courses to familiarize myself with them?"

"Sure, that's a good idea. Go out now if you like because it's slow today. Why don't you begin with the Pacific Dunes course, one of the most popular, and then go over to Old Macdonald which is newer and very unusual," the manager said. Mike was on his way, hopefully, to a new life.

The courses were better and more varied then he could have imagined. He had never been to Scotland, but this place sure looked like his image of the place. Even though he had seen pictures of Bandon, he was surprised by the unique character of the holes, the greens with their pot bunkers, and the short cut turf.

The next day, Mike was ready to go at 7:30 AM. He was not the first caddy to be placed with a group because he was new and had to wait his turn.

At 8:20 he was assigned to a foursome of players from Michigan who had flown into the area the night before in a private Citation Jet. They were thrilled to be there, and gung-ho to play two courses the first day. Another experienced caddy shared the group. It was a great day for both caddies. No stress, bright sunshine and happy people—just what the doctor ordered.

Mike got another unexpected perk from caddying. For the first time his experience as a golf professional was being appreciated. Most of the golfers he was working for had no real knowledge of how to play a true links course. Like the links courses in Ireland and Scotland and some of the courses on outer Long Island, the Bandon Dunes courses play firm and fast and require somewhat different techniques than when playing softer inland courses.

Mike had put together a little speech, similar to what he used to do as a pro, about how to play these types of courses. The golfers lapped up the information.

He would say, "Gentlemen (or Ladies), here are a few tips that I hope will help you navigate these courses at Bandon Dunes, particularly on the days when the wind is blowing a bit. You'll do better if you play your shots more along the ground, using lower ball flights, rather than playing high approach shots to the greens that will be more exposed to the wind and to unpredictable bounces.

"You'll find that most of the holes, like links courses in Scotland, don't have bunkers directly in front of the greens. So when possible, try to use more punch type shots which will land short and run on to the greens. Using more club, play the ball back in your stance a little, choke up somewhat on your grip, keep your weight a bit forward and use a three-quarter swing. That will help you be more in control of your ball flight. When you get closer to the greens, don't always use your lob wedge or sand wedge to pitch with, like at your home course. Instead, try the bump and run shot with lower lofted clubs to get the ball rolling on the ground more quickly. You might even find that chip shots with your hybrid or even your putter will be effective. Lastly, avoid the pot bunkers because they will eat up your ball and waste a lot of shots."

Mike felt he was helping the players with these coaching tips before the start of play, and it probably led to larger tips. The nearly $400 each caddy made most days when they carried two bags didn't hurt either. Every day, Mike's earnings paid a big portion of his rent for the month.

This scenario went on week after week with some days being marred by driving rain coming off the bordering sea. Much to Mike's surprise, many of the golfers at Bandon Dunes played right though rain storms. They said that it was a once in a lifetime trip for them, so what's a little rain. Mike was a happy guy, especially because the caddies were allowed within limits to play the courses, which kept their own games sharp and improved their course knowledge.

21

Agent Hancock was in LA at his desk doing paperwork on May 26 when he got a notice that the search he had ordered on new car registrations had yielded a hit. A 2008 Jeep Wrangler had been purchased by and registered to a George Willis on May 2, in Redding, California. The address given was Bud's old address in LA. Bud finally had made a mistake! The problem was, it didn't get the FBI any closer to catching him because they had no idea where in the US he might be. It did tell Hancock one thing: Bud had gone north.

Joe put the description of the car plus the plate number out with all the police departments in Northern California and asked them to be on the lookout for a blonde male driver in his 30's. He kept his fingers crossed. "This clever bastard could be up in Canada spending the summer on Vancouver

Island for all we know," Joe said to his partner, Paul Clark, sitting across his desk.

"At least it's a piece of the puzzle that we didn't have before," the agent replied.

Special Agent Harry Knight from West Palm Beach was a good Bureau Chief for Palm Beach County. He was also one of the FBI's best golfers. Being 55 years old, six feet tall and in honed condition, he played prestigious senior amateur golf events, in his appropriate age division, whenever he could find one close to the Palm Beach area or somewhere in the southern region that he could fly to in his Cessna.

There were numerous tournaments of this type and they often brought him into social contact with other good senior players. Among the participants, there were many well-off, semi-retired guys who could and would go anywhere to play a great golf course.

One day over lunch, after a morning tournament round, three of Harry's foursome partners were chatting about the great courses they had played and which ones they still had on their radar. Jim Nelson, a retired New York hedge fund guy, said, "One place I've always wanted to play is Bandon

Dunes in Oregon. We tried to put a group together to go last year but it got all screwed up with sickness and one guy's divorce, so it didn't happen.

"How about you, guys? Would you like to see what we can arrange? I have my own plane, a Lear 35 jet, which can take the whole group and we can split the deal."

Charles Bennett, a lawyer, said, "If we can get the dates right, count me in."

Frank Frick, the third man, who owns a series of motel properties in Florida and could set his own schedule, remarked, "I don't care when it is. I want to go with you. That place and Cypress Point have been on my bucket-list from when Bandon Dunes only had two courses and was written about in golf magazines."

They all looked at Harry with anticipation. Harry took a sip of his ice tea and lemonade and told the men, "Look, of course it sounds wonderful and who in their right mind wouldn't be thrilled to go there. But understand, I'm still a working stiff with a bunch of college commitments for my kids' education. It's just not in the cards. But I appreciate the opportunity and the invite to join you. I'm sure you'll find someone to fill out the group."

Jim said, "Harry, we would all love having you with us and we understand your situation, We enjoy your company and our golf games are all about at the same handicap level, so we could have a great time. We could fly out one afternoon, play for two for three days and come back the next morning.

"How about this? If you pay for your own golf fees and food, and if the three of us split the rest, including the airplane and caddy fees, could you possibly do it?"

Harry ran the numbers in his head and said, "My wife will probably kill me but, yes, I could go!" Everybody agreed and set a potential date two weeks later.

"Let's check our schedules and commit within three days and I will make all the arrangements," Jim said.

When Harry got home that night he found out that his wife Jane had made arrangements to go out for dinner with their good friends, Joe Snider and his wife Sharon, to Tiger Wood's restaurant, The Woods, in close-by Jupiter. It's an upscale, popular sports bar with big tv screens, comfortable booths and moderate to expensive food prices.

Harry wanted to speak to Jane about the proposed trip to Bandon Dunes but having Joe listen in might help the discussion. When he told them the story, Jane's first reaction was, "Why in the heck would you want to go all the way to Oregon to play golf when you have hundreds of courses to play right here in Florida?"

Joe Snider just smiled and surely was thinking, "How is he going to explain this?" Joe also played good golf, but was never quite as passionate about it as Harry.

"Well, Jane," Harry said, "I know this might be hard to understand if you're not a golfer, and you're not, so I'll try to give you a broad idea of this unusual situation in the world of golf. At least for those who have the bucks to follow their dreams.

"Thousands of players go each year to the British Isles to play the great courses, such as the Old Course at St Andrews in Scotland, thought to be the home of golf. There are other courses that come to mind, such as Muirfield, that's particularly hard for most golfers to arrange to play. And there's Old Head which is a famous Irish links course with high cliffs bordering the sea.

"Then there are special courses right here in the US that any golfer would give his right arm to play and who would pay any amount of money for an invitation to play, starting with Augusta National where they hold the Masters. But there's also Cypress Point in California, and Pine Valley in New Jersey which has been considered for years by some players to be the best course in the world. Right here in Florida we have Seminole Golf Club which was made famous by Ben Hogan when he practiced there years ago for the Masters. These are all very private courses.

"There is another category of courses that has been made famous because of exposure on TV, that any golfer who can play decent golf would want to play. The Tournament Players Club in the Jacksonville area is one of those, along with Riviera and Pebble Beach in California and Whistling Straits in Wisconsin. Who wouldn't die to play these great courses?

"Bandon Dunes, where we have talked about going, is in the same stratosphere of challenging courses that golfers from all over the world want to experience. Even golfers from across the country are itching to go to this extremely remote place. Playing courses that are characteristically similar to the great courses of Europe, without having to cross the Atlantic, has a great appeal to thousand of avid golfers.

"Let's face it, not everyone can pursue these dreams but there are many passionate golfers at the pinnacle of their careers, or retired with plenty of discretionary money, who can and will go to these places. That's the trip that has been proposed to me. This group of great guys has offered to bring me along for the ride, with only minimal expense. It's an offer I don't want to refuse, so I hope you are in agreement, Jane?"

Before Jane could comment, Joe jumped in and said, "Wow, Harry, that's fantastic. I would go in a minute if I were ever asked, which I won't be of course, because I am not an extremely good player like you."

"Harry, I think it sounds nuts, but if you want to do this and it will make you happy, go for it," Jane said.

The next afternoon, a date of June 9 was set. Destination: Bandon Dunes.

22

Early morning on June 9, the four golfers flew from the private aviation area of the Palm Beach International Airport to Oregon. Talk about the red-carpet treatment! They had it in spades, with drinks and appetizers served by the crew, as well as every magazine or newspaper you could possibly want to read.

Harry said, "This is unbelievable and could spoil me for traveling coach ever again. No check-in, no security, no waiting line. Wow! Thanks for including me, guys."

When they were somewhere over Nebraska, Harry got in a conversation with the pilots about flying. He told them that he owned a four-place Cessna that he used every chance he could. The pilot offered to have Harry sit in the right co-pilot's seat for a stretch to experience flying a jet. Talk about a thrill! Harry was in pig heaven.

By the time they got to the Bandon Dunes Resort and settled in their rooms, it was late afternoon. Not quite cocktail time, but perfect for taking their putters out to the new 100,000 square-foot putting course built by golf architect Tom Doak. It was called the Punchbowl and was unique, to say the least, and free. The guys had a blast and finished in time for celebratory drinks before dinner.

During dinner in the clubhouse, Harry quietly mentioned that he would appreciate no one mentioning that he was an FBI agent because it might make people nervous and take away some of their fun. Everybody agreed and said they understood.

Jim Nelson laid out the plan for the next morning. "We'll be teeing off on the Pacific Dunes course at 8:10 AM. It is the favorite of many players. Two caddies have already been assigned to our group and these guys know their stuff. Then after a quick lunch, we'll play the Bandon Dunes course, the original track that put this place on the map. You'll like them both, although you may not be happy with the scores you shoot because both courses are tough, particularly if there's wind."

"Also, these courses play hard and fast and the turf is cut short, so lofting shots to the greens may not be as effective as bouncing the balls up onto the greens. You'll get the picture after a few holes."

Charles asked, "Jim, can we take carts if we get a little tired? Just asking."

"Sorry, Charles, this is golf the way it was meant to be played. Do you think the Scottish golfer, Old Tom Morris, the 1861 Open Champion, would have ridden a cart, even if there had been such things back then?"

"You've got a point there. We'll handle it," Charles said.

The next morning after a light breakfast, the players gathered at the practice putting green at 7:30 and were joined by their caddies who already had the clubs with them. One older gruff looking guy named Jack was assigned to Jim and Charles. Frank, the motel owner, and Harry were assigned a younger caddy named Mike. After handshakes all around, the group practiced putting and swung a few clubs to loosen up until they were called to the starting tee for the Pacific Dunes course.

When the group was about to leave the putting green for the tee, Mike gave the men his short tip speech. They all thought it was a thoughtful touch on Mike's part and completely in sync with what Jim had warned them about earlier.

The day was unusually calm and a little cool, so the guys were handling the course just fine. They had the six-point game going, and switched partners occasionally. When they finished the ninth hole, they took a short break for soft drinks and a chat which included the caddies.

Jim asked his caddy, Jack, if he had caddied for a while. Jack said, "I've been caddying here at Bandon since the day it opened, and before that I worked on one of the crews that built the first course. You might say, I literally know the place like the back of my hand. I've lived around here my whole life."

"How about you?" Frank asked Mike.

"Well," Mike said, "I'm sort of new here at Bandon. I was a golf pro at one time but couldn't quite cut it, so I figured that caddying would be right down my alley because it keeps me around the game."

Harry asked Mike, "Are you from the Southeast or Florida by any chance, Mike, because you look vaguely familiar to me, but I can't place where I might have met you? Maybe on a golf course somewhere?"

"Nope," Mike replied. "Never spent much time in the Southeast except passing through a few times."

"Hmm," Harry mumbled.

They played the back nine and couldn't stop talking about the brilliance of the design and the natural surroundings. Jim had been to Scotland and Ireland a number of times and told the group that he was impressed with everything he had seen so far. He appreciated the effort that had been made in the construction, including using fescue grasses on the courses, just like the links overseas.

In the afternoon while they were playing the Bandon Dunes course, Harry stole looks at his caddy Mike, trying to place where he had seen him. He couldn't let go of this despite knowing it wasn't really important.

In the middle of the round a small storm system moved through the area and showed the guys just how tough the courses could be with 30-mile per hour winds howling. Pars were not realistic. Bogies were highly welcomed. But they sucked it up using Mike's tips as much as possible, and played though the storm. These conditions were particularly tough on the caddies because many balls were hit into the fescue and needed to be found.

Playing 36 holes in one day was not customary for these senior guys and they would have to do it again the next day, so early to bed was in order. The next morning they would play the Old Macdonald course, named in honor of architect Charles Blair Macdonald, and Bandon Trails in the afternoon.

It was another picture postcard day at Bandon Dunes Resort the following morning. All the players said they slept like babies and were ready to go again. Not Harry.

He had been awake on and off all night obsessing about his caddy. He became convinced they had met somewhere before. When they were walking up the hill to the seventh green of Old Macdonald, Harry casually asked Mike, "Where are you from, Mike?"

"Oh, I grew up in Kentucky," Mike said.

"That's funny," Harry said, "because you don't have that Kentucky twang I know well. I have friends who live there." Mike said that he came from Louisville but had spent a lot of time later on in California.

"I guess I lost the twang over the years."

By the time the group was on the 18th green, Harry had a disturbing thought and couldn't wait to go in for lunch to make a telephone call. When they got inside, Harry excused himself and told the group to go on and have lunch without him because he had an important call he wanted to make. "I'll probably be down from my room in 20 minutes or so," he said.

23

His first call was to his office in West Palm Beach. "Mary, this is Harry calling from Oregon. I need a contact number out of my files for an agent by the name of Joe Hancock in Los Angeles. Could you look it up for me? It should be in the files from that golf ball murder investigation a few months ago."

Mary put Harry on hold and came back in five minutes with Joe Hancock's direct line. Harry thanked her and he immediately dialed.

"Hello, this is Special Agent Joe Hancock, how can I help you?"

"Hey Joe, this is Harry Knight from Palm Beach, Florida calling. You might remember that we talked a few months ago about the bizarre murders that were taking place around the country."

"Yes, I remember you and the situation well. How could I forget that sick bastard with the golf balls?"

"Well, believe it or not, I'm calling from Oregon. I'm here on a golf trip and have met a guy who looks somewhat familiar and I need to see the photo of the suspect again. I believe his name was George Willis. Can you email me a picture of the guy?"

"Sure, happy to. We're damn lucky to have a photo of him. I'll send it in an hour because I have some people about to come into my office."

"Great," Harry said. "I have to go out on the course now anyway so I'll check on things when I get in from playing. I was supposed to be on vacation!"

Harry was able to grab a ham sandwich and an ice tea in time for his group to tackle Bandon Trails, a hilly and challenging inland layout designed by Bill Coore and Ben Crenshaw.

Charles Bennett commented, "We'll be lucky to stand up after finishing this track with all the changes in elevation. Can you imagine having to carry two bags up these hills like Jack and Mike are doing?" Jim said, "Youth is the answer, and don't forget too that money gives them an incentive."

Harry was enjoying every minute on the golf course but his concentration was not focused on his driver or 7-iron. He kept thinking, "What if this Mike guy is really George Willis? What can I do about taking him in? How can I get some other agents or local police to help? If we have to leave in the morning to get home, what will happen then?"

Harry watched every move Mike was making out of the corner of his eye. Everything seemed normal on the surface. Mike was doing his job and was polite to everyone. Mike, though, had sensed Harry's interest in him and picked up that Harry was eyeballing him more than usual. His natural survival instincts were popping to the surface. He thought, "Who is this guy Harry and how the hell would he ever have met me? I don't think he's in the golf business, so I would not have crossed paths with him at the Honda Classic in Palm Beach." Mike asked Jim, as they were approaching one of the last greens, "Mr. Nelson, are you men flying back to Palm Beach tomorrow?"

Jim answered, "That's the plan. I think we've had all the golf our ancient bodies can handle. It's been great and we appreciate the good job you and Jack have done for us."

"We've enjoyed it too," Mike said.

Harry didn't want to be rude, but the only thing he could think about was getting to his room fast, and then checking his email and seeing the photo of George Willis. He excused himself and told his friends he would meet them in the bar shortly. Then he took off.

There on his phone, as clear as day, was a picture of Mike Simmons. This guy was a fraud and a murderer and needed to be taken into custody. Harry called Agent Joe Hancock immediately on his direct line. "Joe, Harry Knight calling. Thanks for the photo. I believe we've got our guy."

"Bud has been caddying in a group I've been playing with for two days. He looked familiar to me, although I had never actually met him in person. I guess I had spent so much time staring at the photo you distributed awhile back, that the image stuck with me. The picture you sent nailed it."

Joe interrupted and said, "This may be a huge coincidence but I got a call about an hour ago from Detective Sherry White from the LA Police Department. She's been involved in this case since the beginning and, in fact, was the person who first called the FBI for assistance. During the last month she has been periodically checking on a postal box that was in George Willis's name, with mail that had never been picked up. Well, she happened to check this morning and found out that the recipient had requested that the mail in the box be forwarded to his name at General Delivery in Bandon, Oregon, a small remote town on the coast."

Harry said, "Guess what, Joe! That's where I am so that confirms the whole deal. Willis is here and working as a caddy at a high-end golf resort called Bandon Dunes under the name of Mike Simmons. He must be living in the small town of Bandon up the road a few miles away. I was thinking that perhaps I should drive over to the town and see where he is living, but that might be tricky and tip him off somehow. I don't want to blow our chances of catching him.

"The question is, how can we handle this so he doesn't get away again? I don't think I should try to do it alone. It's too important that we get him once and for all. I also think that he has probably left the golf course for today because he has already been paid."

"You're right, Harry, we need to capture him alive because our office thinks that he must have killed before this past spree, and that could shed light on who those other likely victims were. This could solve some cold cases we've given up on."

"Ok, let's see if we can come up with a plan," Harry said.

Joe suggested, "I'm sure I can get at least two agents to fly up there tonight and get another agent to come down from Portland or Eugene tonight as well. We'll look for the best place to fly into, where we can get a car or two."

"Here's my situation, Joe. I'm staying at the Bandon Dunes Resort where we have been playing for two days. I'm with three other guys who all flew in together in a private jet. Not my plane, unfortunately. Anyway, we were planning to leave in the morning, but I don't think that it would matter to them if we delayed our departure to make this arrest in the morning. I need to fake this Mike out by making him think our group is going to stay to play another round. Then, when we have him set up, we can arrest him."

"That sounds like a plan that will work, Harry. I'll talk to you tonight as soon as I have organized our people. Talk to you then."

24

When Harry went downstairs he saw his golfing buddies sitting in the bar talking about the two great days they had. The discussion was just turning to when they would leave the next morning. Harry interrupted and said, "Guys, I have to ask your indulgence and cooperation in a ticklish matter. And this is something that I would never speak to you about except that I need your help with this situation in a small way. But this must be between only the four of us, because it's a police matter."

"Ok, Harry," Jim said, "what do you want us to do?"

"Just so you understand, there was a string of murders that took place starting last January. The perpetrator of these horrible crimes has been on the loose for a number of months and it was looking like we would never catch the guy. He was always one step ahead of us. As it so fortunately happened, because you fellows invited me to this remote place, I found myself recognizing a person who I thought should be checked up on. That's why I have been going to my room to make calls so often.

"It's now been verified that the suspect is in fact a caddy working here at Bandon Dunes and who needs to be picked up and arrested. You all know the suspect. He's been caddying in our group for two days. The name he has been going by is Mike Simmons."

"You've got to be kidding," Frank said, "You mean that nice fellow who's been carrying my bag for two days?"

"Yes, that's the guy and believe me he is a clever bastard and could be dangerous. That's why tomorrow morning at least three other FBI agents will be showing up early in the hopes of surrounding and capturing the suspect. What I will ask you to do, Jim, is to go to the caddy master and tell him we want to play one more round on Old Macdonald at approximately 8:00 AM, and that we want the same caddies we've been using. That should get the suspect to come to the facility. Can you do that?"

"I don't see why not. Is there anything else we have to do?" Jim asked.

"Yes, I want you to act normally, just as you did this morning. Speak to the caddies like before. If things go as planned, this can all happen peacefully and quickly and we can get out of here and back to Florida by tomorrow night." They all agreed.

At 8:30 that evening Harry's cell phone rang. "Hello Harry, it's Joe. I think we have things set up on our end. I'll be coming myself with an associate. We're going to take an FBI plane in half an hour. The pilot has the trip planned to get us as close as possible to Bandon."

"We'll also meet up with another agent coming down from Portland. We'll grab a short night's sleep and be at Bandon Dunes by six tomorrow morning. Can you meet us somewhere at that time?"

"Yes, and I suggest you come to the front door of the clubhouse as if you were guests. Dress casually, like golfers with sweaters and the like, so you don't stand out. The suspect will come at about 7:00, but he'll park in an area where employees park, so he will not be able to see you at the clubhouse.

"By the way, my group has been told about the situation and our plans. We were able to get a starting time at 8:00 with the same caddies as today. The suspect should not have a clue that anything is up."

"Good going, Harry, we'll see you at the club at six o'clock."

It was still somewhat dark at six the next morning, but showing signs of daylight in the eastern sky. The air was chilly and it looked like it would be a windy day. Mike Simmons really wanted to stay in bed because the last two days had been exhausting. He hadn't yet gotten his body acclimated to 36 holes two days in a row. He also hated cold windy conditions and looking for balls hit by hackers all over the place. At least his last group was made up of good players and nice guys. He wasn't sure about Harry, but the pay and extra tips made it worthwhile. When he checked in by phone with the caddy master, he found out that the same group wanted him back again for an early round, so he got himself pulled together to be at the course by seven.

Meanwhile, Harry was waiting inside the front door of the clubhouse, hoping to spot Hancock's cars coming down the entrance road. When he saw two cars arrive together he assumed that it was them and went out to greet them and to tell them where to park. He told them to come inside after they parked the cars in the lot and to leave their FBI jackets behind. They truly hadn't gotten the picture about wearing casual golf clothes like a golfer would wear, but Harry figured they would work it out somehow. He brought them into the lunch room and got the men coffee and muffins. The staff gave them strange looks but what could Harry do? He sure couldn't let anybody else in on the plan.

When Mike came into the caddy building, he was shivering and not looking forward to a blustery day. He said to the caddy master, "I appreciate you putting me in a group, but man, I'm beat after yesterday. I'm also surprised these guys wanted to play again. They could hardly walk after playing Bandon Trails."

"I know," said the caddy master, "I was surprised myself because I had put their clubs away in the travel bags when I got the word that they wanted to play once more, and wanted the same caddies. Oh well, money is money."

"Right," Mike said.

For some reason, something nagged at him. He didn't know why, but the pit of his stomach was telling him to be on the alert. He grabbed the two bags that were on the rack near the caddy building and saw Jack who admitted he was also surprised to be going again today. Jack got his two bags and

then he and Mike brought them to the putting green. Everything "seemed" normal.

It wasn't full daylight yet as they passed by the back of the clubhouse. Mike looked into the windows of the lighted grill room to see if the group was having coffee before they came out. What Mike saw was Harry standing and talking with three other men who didn't look to him like they were golfers. Who were they?

Within a few minutes, Jim, Charles and the third guy from yesterday, whose name Mike couldn't remember, came to the putting green and started talking to them in a normal way. They were just yakking and passing the time of day. But Mike felt their conversation sounded a little stilted and forced. He kept looking for Harry to come out. Then he watched him though the window going out of the lunch room towards the front entrance. He thought to himself, "Why is he going that way? What's that all about?" Minutes later, the players put their putters in their bags and said, "Okay, let's go to the tee."

When the group arrived at the 1st tee of Old Macdonald, just a short walk from the clubhouse, Harry came around the corner of the building. About 50 feet behind and off to Harry's side, Mike detected movement near some shrubbery and noticed two of the men he had seen inside. He thought, "Clearly, these men were not heading in the direction of the parking lot and were hiding for some reason. Why would they do that?" His natural instinct alerted him that something was wrong. There was too much unusual activity around the starting tee of this unexpected and unplanned golf game.

25

Over the past months, Mike Simmons was as happy as he had ever been. He was making more than enough money to survive, and he felt useful. He could play golf occasionally on great golf courses and had met co-workers and others who seemed to like him. The thing that particularly pleased yet puzzled him was that his past urges and the desire to do harm to women seem to have dissipated. All he wanted was to be left alone and get his new life in order. No matter what, he wasn't going to jail!

But now he felt tension growing around him. Things didn't seem right. Even the other players in the group looked nervous and twitchy. He made a quick decision — he had to leave right then, even though it would put his job at risk. He grabbed a club from one of the bags, maybe for protection, then started running for the employee parking lot on the other side of the caddy building.

Harry reacted immediately by calling on his radio to ask one of the officers who had car keys to take an automobile to the end of the entrance road and prevent any vehicle from leaving the premises. Then Harry and the other two FBI agents moved rapidly to follow Mike who was nearly 100 yards ahead and getting close to his jeep.

Before Harry could get in a position to stop him, Mike screeched out of the parking lot heading east toward the exit. As he approached the exit, Mike could see the FBI agent's car up ahead blocking his escape. Mike did a U-turn and drove half-way back towards the clubhouse, then turned sharply right into what looked like a dirt maintenance road used for moving equipment between the various courses. The road headed in a northerly direction, but Harry had no clear idea where it might go or if it led to a back exit.

Three golf carts sat next to the caddy building, so Harry called to his men to take one of them and try to keep up as best they could by following Mike's Jeep tracks. Harry, having played the course before, had some idea of the terrain. He grabbed another cart and charged north out onto the golf hole closest to the maintenance road and drove parallel to it, but of course at a slower speed than Mike's Jeep could go.

Mike Simmons was not familiar with all the off-course roads and maintenance areas, and he wasn't sure where the dirt road went. But he discovered soon enough that it only went as far as the most northerly fairway of Old Macdonald. His only choice was to turn west in the direction of the high ridge fronting the ocean on the westerly edge of the course. He couldn't go east because of the impenetrable scrub land and woods. Harry remembered there was a refreshment cottage near the 7th green on the ridge. It surely had an access road out to a public street. Harry saw Mike turn west toward the ocean ridge. Thinking that Mike was heading for the cottage access road to escape, Harry turned his golf cart left to intercept Mike. The

Jeep's speed prevented Harry from getting any closer than about 50 yards.

In less than a minute, after cutting across two or three fairways, Mike entered the curving fairway leading to the seventh green. It was a long uphill grind of a hole with pot bunkers and mounds of all descriptions which prevented a straight up climb. But Mike, having caddied the course, knew the hole well and dodged and darted around the obstacles in his way.

At the top of the hill, over a crest, sat the 7th green with its panoramic view of the rolling waves 100 feet below. There was an extreme drop-off just behind the back of the green. The last thing Harry remembers hearing from the open window of the Jeep was a triumphant yell from Mike. "I'm not ever going to jail!"

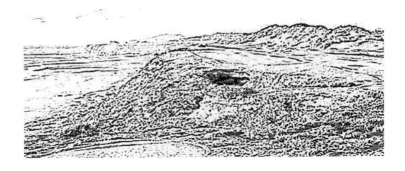

His Jeep accelerated as it came near the top of the crest and careened directly towards the cliff, passing barely left of the green. It reached the edge of the drop-off at about 40 miles an hour and burst out into open space, seemingly suspended before it rolled and tumbled to earth on Whiskey Run Beach below, landing upside down.

The chance of Mike surviving such a disastrous crash was remote. Wanting to reach him as quickly as possible, Harry found the access road from the refreshment cottage to the public road and drove down it with the other golf cart following. The road gave them access to the beach below.

As they drove along the beach and approached the wreck, it was obvious that if Mike was still alive, it would be a miracle. He was hanging out of the Jeep's overturned body and seemed to be partly conscious, still breathing shallowly. He would need immediate trauma care if he was going to survive. But the blood trickling out of his mouth made even a helicopter rescue unlikely to save his life.

As Harry stared into Mike's eyes, he could see that Mike recognized him. The only words that he heard before Mike's eyes closed forever were whispered haltingly. "I'm not going to jail. I changed my life, but now it doesn't matter anymore."

Epilogue

Harry and Joe Hancock knew the nightmare was over but the end was unsatisfactory. They could not interview George Willis to find out what other victims could be identified or how many other women he had killed. They were also disappointed in the way they handled the arrest. He shouldn't have escaped.

If Bud Willis hadn't been so instinctive and alert to the dangers around him, the FBI agents might have overpowered him and taken him into custody within minutes. But Harry Knight knew that would be seen as a sorry excuse by FBI bureau chiefs. Mike's uncommon cat-like instincts had kept him out of the clutches of law enforcement all his life.

Agent Joe Hancock told Harry he had done a great service for the FBI and to all the families of the victims who Bud/Mike had killed by finding him and solving this case. He said, "We'll take care of all the details here. Why don't you guys get in your magic ship and head back to Florida."

Which is exactly what they did. The four golfers were airborne by early afternoon, totally exhausted, but filled with satisfaction for having played a role in the capture of a wanted killer. On board, the crew supplied heavy hors d'oeuvres and celebratory drinks. The guys would have tales to tell their golfing buddies for years to come. The next day at his office, Harry was greeted by a dozen of more agents who congratulated him for his insightful quick action and dedication to his job. It was the trip of a lifetime for everyone, but particularly for Harry.

Detectives Sherry and Charlie in Los Angeles were the first ones to get the word that it was over, and that their efforts had been significant and productive in solving the case. Next, Agent Hancock called Tom Burns of the Houston FBI Bureau and gave them notice to call off any attempt to find Bud Willis.

As news of Bud's death continued to filter though the nation's police departments and FBI regional offices, Joe Hancock began realizing the scope of the effort that had been required to capture and find this murderer. It consumed significant time involving nearly 90 people from coast to coast.

Harry Knight knew that some cynics might say finding Bud Willis was just coincidental, even dumb luck, and that the FBI hadn't located him by normal hard work. Sure, they had at last determined that he had gone to Oregon, so maybe it was only a matter of time before Bud would have been discovered.

If Harry hadn't seen the photo of Bud that was distributed to his office weeks ago, and studied it so intently, which enabled him to recognize the suspect, or if Harry had not been included in the golf trip to Bandon, or if his group had been assigned other caddies, Bud might have survived for years in that remote place called Bandon Dunes.

Whether the conclusion of this case was fate or luck, it was finally over. And for that Harry Knight would take great satisfaction.

AUTHOR BIO

Robert E. Marier grew up Maine and attended schools in Kennebunk, and Groton, Massachusetts.

He graduated from Colby College in Waterville, Maine.

In the early 60's he formed R. E. Marier Inc, a real estate sales and development firm, and became the first developer of retirement and oceanfront condominiums in Northern New England. His major interest was in land use and design.

He has been a competitive and avid golfer all his life, having won three club championships, played in the British Amateur at Troon in Scotland, and has aced 12 holes-in-one.

Bob is an instrument-rated private pilot.

His creative efforts include two US utility patents, two CDs of original studio recorded music, available on line,(Melodies From Maine), and a series of children's electronic musical storybooks, (Murfy Finds A Home).

His current focus is on writing mystery novels.

He is married to Valerie B. Marier, a respected writer, columnist and blogger. They have four children and four grandchildren.

Bob and Valerie live in Kennebunk, Maine and in Palm City, Florida.

Bob's website: bobmarierbooksandsongs.com

This book is the second mystery written within the last year by Robert Marier. His first book, TIDAL POOLS, is a heart-felt yet suspenseful story set in a small fishing village along the southern coast of Maine.

TIDAL POOLS

When the body of a cantankerous lobsterman washes up on a small island in Southern Maine, it sparks controversy, an arrest and unexpected plot twists in the coastal village of Somers Beach.

A recent law school graduate is asked to represent an old friend who is accused of killing a Maine lobsterman. The accused, a black man who once saved the lawyer's life, needed legal help and was adamant that the young lawyer, despite his lack of real world experience, be the one to help him.

Reluctantly, Charles Atkins agrees to defend his friend. His attempt to find the murderer leads to intrigue, frustration and two dramatic trials as well as the discovery of the traditions of lobster fishing in Maine. The story tests the lawyer's faith in his client and himself, and leads the reader on a journey though coastal communities in Southern Maine, Massachusetts and South Carolina. It is suitable for Young Adult readers.

Both TIDAL POOLS and PERFECT FAIRWAYS ... HIDDEN LIES are available at Amazon as Kindle ebooks and Print On Demand books. They are available in local book and gift stores in Maine and in selected club pro shops.

Made in the USA
Middletown, DE
29 June 2019